IT'LL BE
BETTER
TOMORROW

Sylvie Nickels

Cover photo by Sylvie Nickels:
a minor road near the New South Wales-
Queensland border in Australia looking towards
Mount Warning

By the same author
The Young Traveller in Finland, Phoenix House, 1962
The Young Traveller in Yugoslavia, Phoenix House, 1967
Travellers' Guide to Yugoslavia Cape, 1969
Travellers' Guide to Finland Cape, revised 1977
Welcome to Yugoslavia Collins, 1984
Welcome to Scandinavia Collins, revised 1987
The Big Muddy – *a canoe journey down the Mississippi,* Oriole Press, reprinted 2006

Fiction
Another Kind of Loving, Antony Rowe, 2005
Beyond the Broken Gate, Oriole Press, 2007
Long Shadows, Oriole Press, 2010
Village 21, *an anthology of short stories,* 2011
The Other Side of Silence, Oriole Press, 2012
Courage to Change, Oriole Press, 2013

Educational aids
Assassination at Sarajevo, Jackdaw Publications, 1966
Caxton & the Early Printers, Jackdaw Publications, 1968
Scott and the Antarctic Jackdaw Publications, 1971
The Vikings, Jackdaw Publications, 1976

CONTENTS

Acknowledgments

The following stories were published in magazines to whom I would like to make the following acknowledgments:

Countryside Takes* for:** The Wild Wood; ***The Lady *for:* The History Class; ***Scribble*** *for:* Miserere Nobis.

To my very best pal, George, of course, and my friends at Featherton,

past and present

FOREWORD

The seed of an idea for a book often has its origins in one or a series of events which trigger the question "What if ....?" Certainly this has been the case in my novels, several of which arose from exploring the effects of war on the children and grandchildren of participants. My own childhood through World War Two undoubtedly had its influences.

Now in advanced age I have other preoccupations and this anthology reflects some of them. Dementia is something affecting a growing number of families. My husband, George Spenceley, suffered its early stages, in addition to coping with what our doctor referred to as several "health issues". As his sole carer in the last year or two of his life I became aware of a number of factors, including my own regrettable lack of patience. But, above all, I noted that behind the dementia George was still there with his appalling short term memory contrasting with an amazing long term recall.

After his sudden death, I was ill for some time and found a haven in the form of a local residential care home. I also encountered there some memorable old people who had done remarkable things in their lives, and carers who were still doing remarkable things. Unfortunately many residents shared a dislike of hearing aids, which made communication tricky or, at times, impossible.

It is possible that many of us in advanced years are happy enough to live each in our own little bubble, though I wished I had had the skill to persuade them to share their interesting stories with each other, and especially those who did not have the good fortune to have regular visitors or families living nearby.

Instead I have created an anthology of stories whose seeds lie among those residents, their relatives and carers, or in many cases the treasure house of memories from my life with George, my late husband and very best pal. I thank those who set me wondering "What if...?" though all the characters in the resulting stories, with the exception of George, are imaginary.

The title is also George's. Whenever I expressed concern about his health or the future, invariably he responded "It'll be better tomorrow."

WARTS AND ALL

Siobhan d'Arcy turned in through the gates of Manorfields Care Home and, with a few practised manoeuvres, parked her car in its usual place. She glanced at the dashboard clock. Six thirty. At this time of the morning traffic was light, which was one of the reasons she chose to arrive early. More significantly, though, it coincided with the hand-over by the night staff to the first day shift. With the elderly, incidents could happen any time but they tended to occur during the early hours of the morning.

If there were a real crisis in progress, Siobhan stayed overnight. A mercurial mix of Irish and French, she had lost count of the number of hands she had held during the final moments of life. She had read somewhere (was it a Buddhist tenet?) that the most important thing any person could do for another was to help them to die with dignity. And she believed this. Her nine years at Manorfields had taught her that in many cases the elderly had outlived all those who cared – really cared – for them. It was all the more ironical therefore that she had not been there to hold the hand of her husband Louis when he suffered an aneurism in the middle of mowing the lawn ten years earlier. And he hadn't even been elderly.

Before Manorfields, she had been assistant manager at a couple of superior residential homes where she had learned the importance of many details such as fresh flowers on each table of the dining room, regular changes of fresh water in each resident's room, the importance of knocking and waiting for permission to enter each room thus allowing its owner the privacy that was so often lacking in institutions. But she had not warmed to her charges and their expectations and

9

remained on the look-out for a place where she could really make a difference.

And then she heard about Manorfields. It had recently been taken over by a small company specialising in medium-sized care homes. She went to have a look at it before applying for the advertised managerial post. It had once been a small manor house and estate a little way outside the village of Donnington. Most of the manor house was 18th century with a few clumsy later additions and some more recent modernisations. It was an up-and-down sort of place with winding corridors and stairways leading to what had once been servants' quarters. Its main asset was the estate in which it stood. This consisted of a small walled garden beside the house, and then several acres of grounds – mainly lawn but with pockets of woodland and a small market garden area managed by someone called Jacob, cousin to retired local farmer Joseph Forrester.

Over the decades which had lengthened into centuries, the network of roads and Donnington itself had stretched out to touch the Manorfields estate. When the manor was developed as a care home, it was found that the grounds could comfortably accommodate a number of bungalows and eventually block of flats where the more able bodied could maintain their independence until such time as they needed full care.

Siobhan had just taken her coat off in the office when Eleanor came in. She had been the senior carer that night which meant that everything would have been neatly recorded.

"Nothing untoward," she announced cheerfully. "No falls. Half a dozen requests for cups of tea; as many for reassurance for attacks of depression." But as always there had been plenty else to do: the non-stop washing machine catering for the linen in twenty-five rooms, the ironing of residents' clothing, the setting up of trays for breakfast. Eleanor added, "Oh, and Amanda's in the dining room, looking lost."

Round the corner in the dining room, Amanda glanced at her watch. Nearly seven o'clock. She had heard the night staff handing over to the first day shift, and now she sat at a table watching them come and go, taking breakfast trays to residents in their rooms, bringing back their personal laundry.

"You're early, Mandy," Sue, the cook, said as she headed for the kitchen. "Couldn't you sleep?"

Amanda smiled and gave a noncommittal "Mmm."

Sue paused. "I imagine it takes a while to get used to being in a new place." She patted Amanda's arm. "You'll be fine, you'll see."

Amanda hoped so but wasn't optimistic. It had been a bad few months; a bad couple of years. Come to think of it, it had been a bad five years since Don had died quietly in his sleep. It was after that her hearing which had been deteriorating, suddenly plummeted. Weird to think it had become a blessing in disguise once she realised she could do something about it: take up lip reading classes, learn sign language. Amanda had always believed in taking action if you could. The lip reading had transformed her social life. Of course it helped that she had lost her hearing late in life so that the shape of words together with facial expression and body language all helped to make sense of the virtually silent speech that surrounded her. Sign language had more limited benefits since so few people could use it. None of it stopped her missing Donald beyond words.

For a while Amanda had been passed round various members of the family like a parcel, but it became clear that she needed somewhere permanent. A niece had done the research and found Manorfields. The staff were lovely but most of her fellow residents had some form of hearing impairment and communication was limited, not least because several of them spoke in tiny whispery voices. She had moved in three months earlier and was still struggling.

"Hello Amanda." A kindly middle aged figure leaned over her and Amanda recognised the Polish carer. Her name initially had appeared to be something strange like Cloudy when it was spoken, so she had got one of the girls to write it down on the list of carers' names that she was learning so she could address them individually. It turned out Cloudy translated into Klaudia, but somehow the name Cloudy stuck. She was only Polish by origin - her grandparents had come to the U.K. after World War Two and, in due course, had become British citizens.

Cloudy knew quite a lot about deafness as her grandmother had given lip reading and sign classes in Poland; her mother had picked it up and given similar instruction privately at home in the UK. Because she had a deaf friend at school, Cloudy had read up quite a lot about sign language such as the fact the manual alphabet had been in use since the 17th century, and she had learned the basics. She was also well aware that when speaking to someone with bad hearing you should face them and be in the right lighting so that they had a clear view of your mouth. Now she asked "Do you want your breakfast now, Mandy?"

"Yes, please. Just toast, marmalade, coffee, no sugar," Amanda said. She liked Cloudy and, because of her history, found it easy to converse with her. The girl had explained that her work at Manorfields alternated between Activities and Caring. "I like Activities much better," she confided. "Then I take residents into the village or to the Health Centre if necessary. Or I organise a quiz or crossword in the lounge. Caring means cleaning the rooms, or helping serve meals..." It also, Amanda knew, meant being at the beck and call of bells that were buzzed for reasons that ranged from the traumatic to the trivial.

Cloudy continued to the kitchen to get Amanda's breakfast and said to Sue, "She's a really spunky old girl, that Mandy."

"Let's have a bit more respect," Sue said, though not very seriously.

"I have, I have. In Poland we always have respect for old people. We look after them."

Sue didn't bother to point out she was not in Poland now and said instead, "It's her birthday at the end of the month."

"Oh, so will you be doing one of your creations?"

Sue's birthday creations were famous: rich fruit cake elaborately decorated with swirls of coloured icing and just enough candles for an old person to blow out. "Of course. Perhaps we could arrange something for the afternoon," Cloudy said. "It's too far for her family to come. If I'm on Activities that day, I'll organise a Crossword for tea time when you bring the cake in."

Doing a crossword was one of the favourite activities if she gave the residents a choice. She knew this was partly because she amused them, and didn't mind. She had never been an academic in any sense and that, combined with mild dyslexia, meant sometimes she had problems reading out the clues and it was almost as much fun for the residents guessing what these were as providing the right answer to them.

13

Sue reached for the chopping board. "I'm rather hoping that Amanda might team up with Jenny - you know, she's just back from spending the summer with her sister in Devon. Has macular degeneration."

"The one that can't see?" Cloudy looked puzzled. "How will that work?"

"Crosswords. Mandy could read the clues and Jenny has an amazing memory. I heard her quoting great chunks of Shakespearean sonnets the other afternoon. And I've noticed Mandy is often poring over a crossword."

"I'll put them at the same table for lunch," Cloudy smiled. "You old manipulator."

"Who's an old manipulator?" demanded Siobhan arriving breathlessly (she never walked) into the kitchen. "And before you tell me, get me a coffee."

"Cloudy is," Sue said. "She's arranging a meeting of minds."

"Meaning?"

"Getting Mandy and Jenny together."

Siobhan gave this only a moment's consideration before saying, "Of course, Jenny's back from Devon now. Couldn't be a better idea. Put them at the same table for lunch."

Siobhan had nursed both her parents in their final years, and had worked her way through the negative emotions that form the territory of looking after the old and infirm long before she became involved in care homes. She got to know, understand or at least make allowances for their idiosyncracies. There was abrupt Heather, who knew all about trees; Elli with her tales of foreign travels; the impossible Annaliese and her strange friendship with the even more impossible Megan; austere Phillida and her charitable niece; that Ben and his wife who had recently moved into one of the flats; and what about mild little Fran who in her time had joined just about every protest you could think of, in the process acquiring the scars to prove it. And how she had rejoiced over the fast one that old Harry had pulled over those devious Carson twins.

----oOo---

So at lunch time Amanda found herself sitting next to a quiet old lady with short white hair and a benign, if vague expression, who greeted her with "You're new here aren't you? Sorry to ask a silly question, but I've been away and my eyesight is ... well, I'm half blind."

"And I missed some of that because I'm more than half deaf. But say it again slowly; my lip reading is quite efficient."

So Jenny repeated what she said slowly, adding, "My name is Jenny. And by the way it does get better - being here, I mean."

After lunch they found a bench in the shade in the garden. Amanda learned that Jenny was widowed, had had heart problems and then, when her sight began to go, she had moved south from Cumbria to stay with her daughter Brenda. All had been well until Jenny's granddaughter split up with her partner and found herself coping with three children and in need of a job. They had landed, lock stock and barrel, on Brenda's doorstep.

"Wow," Amanda commented.

"Wow indeed," Jenny said, impressed that Amanda had managed to keep up so far. "In fact my granddaughter is very clever with all that digital stuff and landed a good job, so she's the bread winner, Brenda looks after the children."

"And you landed up here," Amanda finished for her.

"It's OK, really."

"Warts and all?" Amanda suggested, and then looked puzzled at Jenny's response. When she had repeated it several times, Amanda said, "It looked as though you said 'Oliver Cromwell'."

"I did. He was covered with them. Warts, I mean."

You learn something every day, Amanda thought. But when she got back to her room, she checked in her Dictionary of Quotations and, sure enough, there it was: the instruction from Oliver Cromwell to the portrait painter Sir Peter Lely that '*I desire you would use all your skill to paint my picture truly like me, and not flatter me at all; but remark all these roughnesses, pimples, warts, and everything as you see me; otherwise I will never pay a farthing for it.*'

She took the dictionary to the dining room at supper time and read it out to Jenny who looked pleased. Afterwards they sat in the conservatory while Jenny excavated her memory for quotations and Amanda checked on her accuracy. As they parted at bedtime she said, "How about we have a go at a crossword," and Jenny's grin was sufficient answer.

The following day Amanda went to the library and settled down to examine the main dailies. The librarian was curious. "Are you going to read *all* those?"

"No, just checking which have the best crosswords."

"I can probably help you there. *The Times* has several at various levels. *The Daily Telegraph* has a good one if you're into cryptics. *The Daily Mail's* is surprisingly challenging."

"Thanks," Amanda said. "I'll settle for *The Times* and its various levels."

She bought a copy from the general store on her way back to Manorfields. Jenny was sitting in the garden, eyes closed, face raised to the sun.

"What was Mark Twain's real name. Seven letters, fourth one 'm'?"

"Clemens," Jenny said without opening her eyes.

By lunch time they had almost finished *The Times 2* crossword. A few residents had wandered past on their morning strolls and admired their zealousness. Stefan, the Polish gardener, paused to chat and gave them the name of an umbellifer they could not recall.

"Perhaps we should start a crossword club," Amanda suggested.

The next afternoon, Jenny's daughter Brenda came to visit and Amanda was invited to join them for tea.

"And how about your family, Amanda?" Brenda asked.

"Two sons, one daughter, four grandchildren, scattered round the four points of the compass. Nearest one is a grandson at London University."

"You can borrow some of mine," Jenny said. "I don't know what I'd have done without them when my Bob died." Amanda knew that had been five years earlier. The fact that they had both experienced the lonely vacuum that was bereavement had contributed in no small way to the bond forming between them.

The regular sessions with Jenny helped no end, but Amanda was not sure she could ever settle to the routine of what was, however kindly run, an institution.

Her room was on the first floor from which she looked down on the walled garden and could watch some of the residents diligently taking their daily exercise - and the staff sneaking out for an unobtrusive smoke.

When she had time, Cloudy did a crossword or a quiz in the lounge, and once a week, there was a flower-arranging demonstration. But there still seemed acres of time in which to think of all the plans she could no longer make with Don nor hear him say when she returned *'So come and tell me all the news.'* She had his photograph where she could see it from her bed, and talked to it regularly. The trouble was that there never was any news, and she could not visualise there ever would be. And it seemed that most of the other residents felt the same way since the conversation rarely ranged further than the state of the weather and what day it was.

On the morning of her birthday, Amanda awoke at five o'clock with a sense of premonition that was like a clenched fist in her midriff. Of course, it was not the first birthday since Don had died. There had been five of his, and now this was her fifth. And four Christmases. But it was the first birthday in which there seemed no purpose in having any more. Earlier ones had been spent with family or friends who had done their best to fill the time with activity and her mind with distraction.

She rang the bell. Cloudy was on night duty and came in with a cup of tea without being asked. She stayed a few minutes.

"It is your birthday," she said.

"A bit pointless," Amanda returned without meaning to.

"You've had a good life, made someone happy. Not everyone has done that," Cloudy reprimanded.

"Now you maybe lonely, but not pointless. Look how good you are for Jenny. And she is for you." She plumped up Amanda's pillows. "This afternoon we shall have a crossword."

"Thank you Cloudy. I look forward to it."

Amanda spent the morning in the garden reading. She hoped Jenny would make an appearance and was disappointed when she didn't. Nor was she there at lunch time. The post brought a few birthday cards from family and friends and Amanda spent a lot of time arranging them on her chest of drawers. Then at three o'clock she went to the lounge. Unusually Jenny wasn't there, arriving breathlessly at the last moment as Cloudy was reading out the first clue.

The small trays of tea had been handed round to everyone when Sue came into the lounge preceded by the enormous cake she was holding: two layers of it cascading with clouds of pink and white icing. She brought it to Amanda and gave an elaborate curtsey as she said "Happy Birthday, Mandy." Then she set to and cut the cake into portions which two carers handed round.

To Amanda's surprise the other residents barely took any notice of the cake, but one by one made their way, some leaning on sticks or wheeled frames, over to where Cloudy was sitting at the piano. As they positioned themselves in a group beside it, she began to play *'Happy Birthday to You',* and to Amanda's astonishment, the residents mimed the lyrics, not exactly in time, but unmistakeably the right words. Cloudy caught her eye and winked. Clearly she had taught them. Even Jenny. It must have taken enormous concentration, given her lack of eyesight.

Amanda felt a tightening in her throat and a pricking behind the eyes. Jenny moved away from the group and came over to give her a hug.

"It'll be all right, Mandy. You'll see."

Amanda hugged her back. "Of course it will," she said. "Warts 'n all."

THE WILD WOOD

"She's in the garden," Siobhan, told Joseph Forrester as she met him in the hall of Manorfields Care Home. She, Heather Armitage was always in the garden on fine days. He went on through the dining room and the conservatory to look for her. There she was in one of the furthest corners listening to music through those earplug things. Since her eyesight had got worse she listened to music a lot.

He said quietly, "'Afternoon Missis," so he wouldn't wake her if she were asleep. When she didn't respond, he sat at the other end of the bench and thought back, as he often did, to the strange circumstances that had brought them together.

It had been about ten years earlier. As he studied a young ash critically Joseph Forrester had caught himself humming. He stopped, grunted. Hadn't hummed since Maggie died and that would be seven years tomorrow.

There wasn't a day he didn't think of her, but the thinking was never so hard when he was outside, practising what he had learned over nearly 70 years of working with nature.

"Reckon if you stood still long enough you'd grow roots," Maggie used to tease him.

They'd both wanted a kid but it wasn't to be. He guessed she really minded too, but they'd each kept it to themselves. Then much later she'd suddenly got thin. They didn't talk much about that either but he'd done his best for her those last five years. While she could, she'd quite often come to the gardens at Langham Grey where he worked for the Major. When the pain got too bad they put her in the hospital and she'd slipped away while he was holding her hand.

He took to working from dawn to dusk, but the time came three years ago when even he recognised it needed a younger man. The Major said "You'll always be welcome at Langham Grey, Joseph. After all you made these gardens."

He soon stopped going, though, unable to stomach the new-fangled short-cut ways of doing things. It was the worst time in his life, waking up to long purposeless days. Things got a bit better once he took over the allotment, and then the one next to it, but he still kept himself to himself. At midday he went across to the Red Lion but an hour was enough and he didn't invite conversation. And the village was changing so much: the bakery and butcher's shop went, replaced by a hairdresser and a dentist; the village store turned into a mini-market; and the old folks' club closed down. He blamed the incomers who shopped in the big supermarkets and had gradually taken over the village with their play reading groups - whatever they were - and theatre outings.

Like that Mrs Armitage who was into everything. Apparently she had spent a lot of time in that third world place. Once in the village shop she'd had the nerve to ask him if he could spare a couple of hours to sort out her garden.

"I don't do folks' gardens," he'd said curtly and turned his back on her.

Now he said sharply "Get on with it you old fool," and gently but firmly took his pruning knife to the young ash.

It was the Major who had told him, "I hear they're planting a wood down by the river. I'm sure they'd appreciate your expertise."

But no one had asked Joseph his opinion. Whirling Wood they'd called it. In the Red Lion he picked up the odd snippet. "That Mrs Armitage is organising a wild flower planting day."

"Them environment people are building an otter holt by the stream."

"The mink'll find it first," Joseph couldn't resist saying.

Four years later, after the Millennium, his curiosity eventually got the better of him on a fresh early summer morning. He had been torn between delight and fury. Delight at the shimmer of young growth and the tangle of ragged robin, buttercup and oxeye daisy in a clearing by the stream; fury at the neglect of the trees themselves. A line of willow saplings bowed low and unattended in the path of the prevailing wind. Not a single tree had been pruned to give it shape and grace in decades to come. It was a long time since he had felt such outrage.

Too late to do anything then. But come the following winter ....

----oOo----

From all the gossip he picked up at the pub, he knew Heather Armitage wasn't very popular in Donnington although she had done quite a lot for the village in the years since she chose to retire in it. Nevertheless it was hard to believe anyone would deliberately sabotage Whirling Wood to spite her. The fact was that the wild wood for which she had fund-raised, fought and laboured to make a reality a mile out of the village, appeared to be under siege.

Now in their fifth winter, the trees were being systematically pruned, her beloved infant wild wood tamed. It was intolerable. Of course, Joseph knew very well what was happening and he certainly wasn't telling.

"It must be a nutter," a visiting friend suggested to Heather Armitage whose lips pursed in disagreement.

The friend glanced at her intelligent, uncompromising expression and thought how interesting that a small green dot on the Midlands map could acquire such importance to someone who appeared to have it all.

She suggested "You need a sleuth. What about that pale boy with the black dog we met down there? With a funny name - Spud I think you said. Lives on the new housing estate."

Later, Joseph heard from the gossip in the pub that Mrs Armitage had gone to see Spud to ask him to keep an eye on the wood. "When you take your little dog to Whirling Wood," she had added.

"Blackie's run over," was Spud's reported response, adding "Dead" in case he hadn't made himself clear.

"Oh," Mrs. Armitage said. A pause, then "I'm very sorry."

To break an awkward silence Spud blurted out "But, like, I can go for you anyway."

"*Could* you? Could you go every day for a while - say, for 50p a time?"

Spud stared at her in amazement. He was to be *paid* for going to his favourite place! Already he had forgotten his vow never to go there again now Blackie was dead.

Mrs Armitage said he was to look out for someone who was cutting off branches; and if he could tell her who it was, there would be a fiver for him.

So, one February afternoon, Spud had gone to Whirling Wood on his own. The late afternoon sunshine slanted low over the young trees making silvery sparks of the early catkins and gleaming blood red on the dogwood stems. With no Blackie the thing Spud noticed was the stillness.

A stillness broken by the crackle of twigs underfoot and a faint tuneless humming.

Spud crept on. Oh *crumbs,* it was that horrible old Mr Forrester who used to shout at Blackie for digging holes. Without warning, he gave an explosive sneeze.

Old he might be but Joseph Forrester's grip on the scruff of Spud's neck felt like a steel clamp.

"Leggo," he yelled.

The old man glared at him. "Oh it's you, is it?"

If he legged it home the old man would never catch him. Then all he had to do was report to Mrs Armitage, collect his fiver and go. But Spud felt oddly cheated: all those 50ps - and he'd gone and solved the mystery in one go. He was also curious.

He mumbled "Wondered, like, why you're cutting all them branches off."

It was a long time since anyone had shown any interest in what Joseph Forrester did. He also remembered hearing in the Red Lion about the dog, and said gruffly "Not any old branches; just particular ones so the tree will grow straight and strong."

Spud was puzzled. Mr Forrester didn't look at all as though he'd been caught doing something he shouldn't. "So that's a good thing, isn't it?"

"Of course it's a good thing," the old man said impatiently. "Been doing it all my life, helping things grow strong, making everything look better."

Spud's puzzlement grew. It sounded great. So what was Mrs Armitage on about? He said "Could you teach me?"

Something seemed to constrict Joseph's throat and he cleared it noisily. "Too late to start now. Come after your tea tomorrow."

Over the next afternoons Spud was down at Whirling Wood as soon as he'd swallowed his last mouthful of tea. Joseph Forrester heard him long before he came into sight and was surprised how glad he was; and how much he missed him the times he had to stay home for a visiting relative.

He worked methodically, explaining to Spud what he was doing. Sometimes he'd ramble off into long stories of how everything in nature was linked, and the way plants and insects and animals had learned to work together. Spud didn't understand a lot of it, but he liked the idea of so much unseen order. Sometimes they'd end up with a short circuit of the wood, looking at insects and things. Twice they saw woodpeckers, and once the flash of a kingfisher along the stream. And the old man told him a lot about the wild flowers.

----oOo----

Heather Armitage printed out her latest editorial for the Donnington News thoughtfully. She had assumed Spud had simply got bored and given up on his undertaking until his mother happened to mention that morning his daily eagerness to get down to Whirling Wood. In Heather Armitage's limited experience, small boys did not forego a daily 50 p without good reason. She reached a decision.

She saw the two figures from some distance away: Joseph bending to examine an oak sapling, Spud hunched beside him. Joseph Forrester, one time Head Gardener at Langham Grey!

Spud looked up and said. "Oh cripes."

Joseph straightened. And said nothing.

26

"So perhaps you would care to explain Mr Forrester," Heather Armitage said coldly.

"S'all r-right," Spud blurted, stammering in his anxiety to reassure her. "Mr Forrester, he knows all ab-bout looking after t-trees."

"I'm well aware of Mr Forrester's skills, thank you Spud. I merely wish to know why he is exercising them on my ... our wild wood."

"Wild wood!" Joseph said scornfully. "Takes a thousand years or more to make a wild wood. And who heard of a wild wood with a parking place and a made-up a path!"

They glared at each other. Heather Armitage's next thought was that this strange old man had voiced her own deepest reservations about paths and parking places; and then that he actually seemed to think he was repairing some awful neglect.

She said "We're *trying* to make it a wild wood. Trying to think of the next thousand years. Get back some of the wildflowers and mammals and insects we've lost."

Joseph thought, *she talks real queer, but there's some sense in it.* He said "There were Banded Damselflies near the brook last summer."

"Indeed there were Mr Forrester," Heather Armitage said. "And a few Beautiful Damselflies too. These are just the habitats we must protect as well as re-create others we've destroyed."

Joseph grunted. "Won't be no wood if you don't tackle them rabbits," he said nodding at the oak sapling.

Heather crouched down beside him. "Oh dear. What do you suggest?"

Spud looked from one to the other in growing astonishment. He'd never understand grown-ups.

27

"It's them plastic guards, a lot of them aren't fixed properly." Joseph's tone implied *what else could you expect from a bunch of amateurs?*

Heather straightened up, looked round in the fast fading light. He was right.

She was not one to hesitate. "I suppose Mr Forrester you wouldn't consider taking charge of checking them ..."

"Big job," Joseph said.

"I'm afraid as a charity we couldn't offer..."

"It's not money I want Mrs," he interrupted impatiently. "It's more hands – like this young'un."

An idea was gaining rapid appeal. "You recruit who you like Mr Forrester. But only on the understanding that they take their orders from you." Heather Armitage considered a moment. "You could, in fact, be our official warden." A small pause. "Only no more pruning. "

Joseph looked her straight in the eye. "You don't never prune a wild wood," he said.

----oOo----

Watching Spud grow from childhood into young adulthood, she sometimes regretted that she didn't have someone to whom she could pass her enthusiasms. Once when she coincided with him down at the wood, she started to telling him about her times working in Africa and Asia. He proved a surprisingly receptive audience, then told her he planned to travel the world himself. She found herself telling Joseph about it. After a grunt or two he said, "Me and my Maggi wanted kids, but wasn't to be." And then some time later he added, "She said, my Maggi did, that all them growing things were our children.

Well, it was an interesting way of looking at it. It was a long time later that Joseph presented her with a map. "Look, Missis. Our wood." It took a while to understand, until she saw it was a new edition of a map of their area. And there, close to the cluster marked as Donnington, was a patch of green bearing the words 'Whirling Wood', "Last longer than kids," Joseph said. No point in saying that kids had kids, generation to generation. Jess studied the green patch on the map that had not been there before and felt a warm glow

A few years later, the old girl had broken her hip, then her eyesight began to go. Joseph had found her wandering around Whirling Wood, looking lost, so he had taken her home, then shown her his allotment. It turned out she knew quite a lot about growing things. so it became a habit that she would go to visit his allotment, at first quite often, then gradually from time to time. Sometimes Spud would be there, giving Joseph a hand after school. After her hip operation she moved into Manorfields care home and he would go and visit, sometimes bringing a bag of fresh veg.

On a nice day he'd taken her out in a wheelchair, and even occasionally they made it to the allotment. She always noticed any changes he had made.

Now, he was brought back to the present by her voice, "Good afternoon, Mr. Forrester. How pleasant to see you."

They talked, as they always did, about his allotment, the state of the countryside, the latest news of some good or ill inflicted on it by humanity.

"And our wood?" Heather Armitage asked.

"It's doing fine, Missis," Joseph said, "Our wood is."

WAKE UP CALL

The Carson parents could not have been more friendly and pleasant, which was why it was so difficult to tackle them about their dreadful twins. Twice a week they visited Doris, Madge Carson's mother at Manorfields Care Home and, because Madge's mother refused to wear her hearing aid, they turned to Harry Briggs for conversation instead. After all they had been neighbours for a dozen years.

Harry had been at Manorfields for nearly a year. He had befriended Doris because she was quiet and didn't encourage conversation. They would sit in the lounge, reading and trying to ignore the television that was almost permanently on at full volume. Then she had suggested it would be more peaceful reading in one of their rooms, so they did which was why he was usually there when her daughter came to visit. All in all he had settled in quite well, as much as you could settle down after everything you regarded as normal in life had been turned upside down. Even the dreadful twins had been part of that normality - and it looked as though they would continue to be.

The Carsons had become Harry's neighbours a couple of years after he and Elsie moved in to what she described as their retirement haven, and weren't they so lucky to live in such a nice area when money had got a bit tight and they had to down-size. Jack Carson managed a D.I.Y. store in town and Madge worked part time at the local health centre. She was clearly pregnant and in due course produced the twins. Elsie presaged they might be trouble from the time they began to toddle. The problem started when they were six or seven: broken glass on their patio, loose panels in the dividing fencing. Mild vandalism you would call it: nothing he couldn't repair or replace, but it left him with a sense of invasion.

As they got older they became bolder: Baz with his shaved head and earring, and Jos with her tongue stud and the tattoo across her lower back. They'd see his bathroom light go on and know that, whatever he heard, by the time he got downstairs again they would be well away. He loathed the slowing down which meant the garden was getting – had got – in a mess. No point in seeing doc. He knew what he would say: *well, at 89, what do you expect?*

At some point Harry noticed they had been into his shed. He kept meaning to put a lock on the door, but it all seemed such an effort. No damage, but a funny smell, as though they'd been smoking. But they weren't really doing any harm. Nothing was missing, though they probably wouldn't be tempted by well-used garden tools and broken bits of household equipment. But he didn't mention it to Elsie as she would only have worried.

Why did they do it? He had watched some of those documentaries they put on about alienated youth. Apparently they were bored.

Dear God – bored! When he wasn't very much older than Baz was now, Harry had joined the RAF straight from school. He wasn't one of those who said they needed another war to sort the youngsters out. Well, truthfully, he was but Elsie had argued him out of it. Only she'd left him five years ago. Died in her sleep just like that. Mixed up with his grief was anger. Women were supposed to live longer than men. Everyone knew that.

A few months later he succumbed to the barrage of advice from his daughter Beth and agreed to move in to Manorfields. Truth was that he missed Elsie abominably and the daily silence was hard to live with. The staff at Manorfields were marvellous and there was quite often some kind of activity, like a quiz or bingo or musical entertainment, or some outings in the summer.

Nevertheless he noticed early on how much the residents relied on visitors to break up their days. He started reading more and it was then he befriended Doris. One problem was keeping up contact with the family and friends as he didn't like to bother the carers for use of the cordless telephone. So Beth bought him a mobile. His grandson Billy had spent most of a day showing him how to use it, proud as anything to be the one in charge for once. And then he'd insisted on ringing Harry regularly to test his grandfather on the mobile's various features. A few months ago he insisted his mother replace it with a new model as the old one was 'so yesterday'.

It wouldn't last of course. Billy would grow up, find new friends, and get bored with his granddad's old fashioned ways. Perhaps he would even shave his head, wear an earring, become one of a gang.

Pray God, no.

When Madge's mother died, the Carsons became his regular visitors. Unfortunately they always brought the twins who liked to come because Manorfields had extensive grounds just right for young people who still enjoyed war games. Madge clearly worried about them. She laughed apologetically about their appearance, saying "I'll be glad when they grow out of it." She sighed. "But I do worry about them a bit – so much time spent up in their bedrooms at their computers with these – what d'you call them – chat groups. But they're good kids, always looking out for each other."

And then things started disappearing from Manorfields: just small things, like a purse or a pair of glasses or a pen. It wasn't so much the value as the nuisance these disappearances caused. Harry had a shrewd idea why they were disappearing. After a while he had a plan which involved his almost state-of-the-art mobile phone, and that trick Billy had shown him. The next time the Carsons visited, he left his mobile casually on a small table near the sofa. When they had gone, so had the mobile. Now he could only hope he had got the timing right.

Two days later, the Carsons arrived on schedule. "You all right, Harry?" Jack asked. "You look bothered."

"Yes, yes. Well, no not really. I seem to have mislaid my mobile."

"Oh dear," Madge said. "You've just put it down somewhere. It must turn up."

"Do sit down, Harry." Jack pulled a chair over. "You look a bit shaken up."

"I suppose I could have left it at the Co-op when I went to get the paper."

Jack stood looking helpless. "Tell you what, I'll nip over and check for you. Presumably you've checked with the carers here?"

"They've turned the place upside down." Harry took a surreptitious glance at his watch. Five o'clock. Oh, he did hope he'd got it right. And then, right on cue, a jaunty musical sound began to emanate from the baggy pocket of Jos' loose-knit jacket in startling pink. She pulled something out of it and dropped it as if she'd been bitten.

They all stared at the small silvery instrument lying on the carpet, flashing and jangling. After a moment Harry picked it, pressed a button or two and there was silence. The silence that followed seemed to go on for a long time.

Then "Wicked," Baz said.

"Maybe, but where does it come from?" Jack demanded.

"I…" began Jos.

"She found it under a hedge near the Co-op," Baz said quickly. As he caught Harry's eye there was mutual recognition that this was a patent lie and, on Baz's part, a grudging admiration for an out-manoeuvring opponent.

"I'm afraid it's a bit wasted on me," Harry confessed. "Too many gimmicks."

Jos visibly perked up. "We could probably work it all out for you if you like. We like a challenge don't we Baz?"

"Yeah," Baz said.

"If it's challenges you're after I can offer you quite a few," Jack said. "Like turning our jungle back into a garden."

"Now that *is* a good idea," Madge said. "Get you some fresh air and exercise, instead of being glued to those computers."

"I could show you some real stuff," Harry offered. "Bit of parachute from when I baled out in the war…"

Jos' eyes widened. "Were you in that old war. One of those fighter pilots?"

"Bomber Command actually."

"But that was history!" Baz exclaimed.

Harry smiled. "I am history," he said. He thought of something. "But some quite interesting things happened, like when I was a prisoner of war."

Jos sat up. "You were a prisoner of war? Wow! Would you tell us about it?"

34

Harry thought a moment. "A lot of people here had interesting adventures in the war. And in different parts of the world. Perhaps some of your friends might be interested, too." It would do the old folks a power of good to get a bit of young company.

"Not to mention their parents," Madge added.

"Mm," Harry said. "It'll be thirsty work. We'll probably need some beer." He turned to glance across at Baz and winked. And it wasn't his imagination that Baz winked back.

THE HISTORY CLASS

In the dining room at Manorfields, several tables of bridge players were in concentrated groups, as usual on a Saturday; a number of people came in from the community to play with the residents. I knew Jess would not be among them. She was waiting for me in the garden, the furthest, quietest corner. Her nose was buried in a book though I doubted she could see enough to read much of it. Something about the way she held herself reminded me of a different Jess from the past. Though no doubt I was different too.

"I've joined a history class," she had announced at a Sunday lunch about two years ago. "Wednesday evenings. Before my brain totally atrophies." She didn't need to add *since I moved in next door.*

Jess, Jessica Bilham, Greg's arty widowed Mum, an amazing 88 years old. We'd moved to Donnington soon after Greg's retirement to be near her. Greg had taken to "just popping over to see if she needs anything" and Thursday had become his Jess-day, part of life's routine like the weekly supermarket shop. Except for the occasional outing I managed to exclude myself from these encounters. We just hadn't clicked Jess and I.

"I don't see the problem, Shona love," Greg said. It's always *Shona love* when he professes I baffle him. "Jess is forever on about how marvellous it is the way you cope with home, and kids, and me, and part-time job" (in the local health centre) "and all those charity involvements" (two actually).

He never had understood it was the *way* she went on about it that made it quite clear I scored zero as a daughter-in-law when it came to creative talent which, of course, was what Really Counted. Because I knew he adored Jess I let it go. And with the length of a largish village between us it hadn't been important for quite a while.

And then she had started falling about and Greg had said "That's the third fall this week. The house is much too big, and anyway she shouldn't be on her own."

There had followed a silence in which I knew I was supposed to say "She could come and live with us." But I didn't, knowing in that far-back bit of my mind where unacknowledged things lie, this was something I had always dreaded.

Greg put his arms round me. "The obvious thing would be to move her into the care home next door. She already has a couple of acquaintances there, the rooms are pleasant, the food good and the staff angelic."

Which was all very well, but she'd be there with her disapproval, permanently just the other side of a wall.

"The twins will be glad," I said, and knew I'd given in.

Ben and Becky, aged ten, were the progeny of our daughter who had moved to Australia, married, moved back to the UK and settled within ten miles of us following a divorce. The children went to Donnington school, had supper with us, and probably spent as much time with us as with their high-flying mother who had carved a rather good career for herself in local television. They adored Jess who insisted we all called her that rather than Gran because "it keeps me young."

Decision finally taken, Jess set about disposing of her huge furniture and her too-big house without, it must be said, a trace of self- pity. And in Spring 2013 she moved in next door. One of her architect friends turned a derelict outhouse in our garden into a studio with a tiny conservatory "where", she announced, "I can unfold in the morning sun." Somehow she reached an arrangement with Manorfields that she came and went as she pleased as long as we took full responsibility for her medication and hospital visits.

It was OK at first. Apart from joining us for Sunday lunch and materialising in her studio most days, Jess didn't really intrude on our daily lives. Rather it was the other way round.

"Why can't Jess eat with us every day?" Ben demanded very soon.

Greg avoided my eye. "She likes to be by herself. And you're *not* to pester her."

They did, of course, bursting in on her as soon as they got home from school. And Greg wasn't much better with his "just nipping over to see if she wants to go back next door," most evenings after supper. All of which meant that I did not have to get too involved.

"What's achoffies?" Ben wanted to know now.

"Atrophies. Sort of shrivels up. Like your brain will if you don't do your homework," Greg said. "Did you say that history class was on a Wednesday? If so, that's the one evening I'm late home."

Jess said briskly "I'm perfectly capable of walking a few hundred yards to the village hall."

The tutor, James, was a retired academic who'd moved to the area from nearby Brum. Jess was delighted with him and his class. Then on the third Wednesday she tripped as she was leaving the village hall.

James brought her home by car, cross and bruised but otherwise undamaged. "She really shouldn't be walking on her own," he said sounding sharp.

"Stop fussing James," Jess said "I'll use that infernal stick the doctor keeps wittering on about."

I heard myself say "I'll take you."

"That's that then." James stopped sounding sharp and beamed at me. "There are a couple of vacancies on the course if you want to join us. No obligation of course."

I had absolutely no intention of doing so, but when I delivered Jess the following Wednesday and James said "Why not stay, see what you think?" I couldn't quickly produce a convincing reason why not.

History was not a subject I'd given much thought to before. The complexities and demands of here-and-now seemed quite enough to be getting on with. But James certainly had a way with him. Quite unexpectedly and absorbingly in the next two hours, I got the first glimmerings of how the past was as relevant to the present as the present was to the future: that we were all miniscule cogs in the wheel of time; that today was tomorrow's history.

Somehow it was taken for granted that I'd stay on for the course, and I found I didn't mind. Jess had found a soulmate called Anne from a neighbouring village and made it clear she would continue sitting with her at the front of the class. That left me to skulk unnoticed at the back, which was fine by me.

James was concentrating on a general history of our area, most particularly because we were approaching Donnington's millennium in 2016. He wanted us, he explained, to look at our surroundings with new eyes: observe old field boundaries, tell-tale humps marking deserted farms; ferret out the original lay-out of the village. The twins had recently got interested in the Vikings - I suspect the horned helmets were the main attraction - so I took special note on learning that Donnington actually straddled the old frontier between the Viking-settled areas and the Anglo Saxons. When I imparted this nugget of knowledge to the twins Ben said airily "Jess has already told us all about that."

Becky added "Have you noticed how her brain has stopped shrivelling?"

I tried to discuss the odd historical point with Jess, as one student to another as it were; but she was not encouraging.

About half way through the course James produced the idea of turning Donnington's millennium into a proper celebration. "A sort of DNA of Donnington," he elaborated. "Old diaries, parish records, maps, photographs, prints - everything that combines to make Donnington uniquely what it is."

It would need a lot of research, he went on, and should keep us fully occupied up to 2016 when the aim was to display our findings in a special exhibition for all to see ("If I'm still alive," Jess muttered"). James even persuaded the Parish Council to cough up a contribution to buy proper display boards

"But I need a coordinator," James concluded. "And I'd like to suggest Jessica whose knowledge of the area and artistic flair will be invaluable."

There was a general rumble of agreement. Jess was obviously chuffed to pieces.

"And Shona." Suddenly all eyes swivelled in my direction as James addressed me across the class. "If you could be available for a bit of chauffeuring ....?"

"Anne's already offered," Jess said firmly, belying Anne's startled look, "And she's a wizard with a computer, which means we can start out with a proper

40

data base." Since when did Jessica know about data bases?

Why was it that, instead of feeling let off the hook, I actually felt rather miffed?

The effect of the project on Jess was remarkable. "As if she's been given a completely new lease of life," Greg said.

The twins complained her brain had become so big and busy perhaps it would be better if it shrivelled again meaning that she no longer lavished so much time on them. Indeed she was out and about all over the place, usually with Anne in tow, checking this museum or that library. And when she wasn't, there was a steady flow of telephone calls or visits from other members of the class delegated to fulfill various tasks.

By the end of the second year's course James had superficially covered Donnington's life story. "We'll be looking at its more important chapters in detail during the next terms," he said. In the meantime the last class before the holidays would become our own personal update: Donnington within our times, seen through our eyes and according to our experience.

I wondered if he'd really thought that idea through. A lot of the class were relatively new to the village - that is within the last twenty years which is extremely new by Donnington standards. Indeed, apart from a few farming families, Jess - fourth generation born and bred - was the only Donningtonian in the fullest sense.

Not surprisingly the reminiscences got off to a slow start. There were predictable contributions about how attractive the village and its setting were, and the general joys of the countryside. Then a peevish note was struck as one or two started homing in on the lack of facilities for the youngsters, the ever-decreasing shops, the limited public transport. I could see James was beginning to regret the idea.

Then into a quiet lull came Jess's voice. She had a good voice and spoke thoughtfully, almost as if reminiscing to herself which, in the end, I realised was exactly what she was doing. And before long any fidgetting or shufflng of papers ceased.

"In 1942 there was just a dusty lane," she said. "The main road was five miles further than it is now. It took the fire brigade and ambulance an hour to get here that morning the bomb fell. I suppose it was just a Jerry wanting to get rid of his load before he headed for home. Anyway it was a direct hit and Father was home on leave and killed outright. Mother and I were out in the fields. Just a few scratches, but I remember the terrible noise and everything crashing down and the dust. I was in my teens." She paused for a few moments, obviously collecting herself, then went on. "Soon after I joined up and trained to be a fanny."

There was a ripple of puzzlement from the audience and Jess smiled. "Yes, sounds a bit bizarre doesn't it? But it was an acronym for FANY and stood for First Aid Nursing Yeomanry. Rather surprisingly, despite its name, I found myself training as a wireless operator and we did really quite important stuff, like sending coded messages to agents we'd dropped behind enemy lines. Very hush-hush."

What a lot I still didn't know about this tough old bird.

"It's true public transport was better after the war than now; for a start, there weren't all those cars. But we did a lot of walking. Three miles each way when I graduated to the Senior School. And of course you don't miss what you don't have so instead of TV we had darts, and pingpong - in this very room come to think of it; and local hops - our version of the disco; or went bluebelling or blackberrying or mushrooming. There was the village fair twice a year until no one had time to organise it any more. so they reduced it to once, then did away with it altogether."

She must have gone on for a full quarter of an hour, and I could actually visualise a Donnington I'd never known. And now I was visualising a Jess I'd never stopped to think about: a young Jess who'd worked her way through art school without a Dad and, in due course, brought up a son without a husband. Greg's father had died in an accident when Greg was eleven.

A year older than the twins.

Some years ago I'd chanced upon a file of cheap greeting cards and calendars that Jess must have produced when she needed every penny she could earn. It hadn't occurred to me at the time but, knowing her bold (and for me difficult) abstract style, I guessed how she must have hated doing them. Of course she would never have let on to Greg.

And what else wouldn't she have let on? That she didn't want other people completely taking over her life, popping in every other minute, giving her lifts, requiring her to be grateful?

"It wasn't easy for someone as dreamy as I was," she was saying now. "Young women nowadays are so well organised, so sure of themselves. I really envy them because I just seemed to flounder from one thing to the next. Still we must have known what we needed to do, and did it, and we survived." She stopped quite suddenly; there was a small silence, and then a ripple of sound grew into enthusiastic applause. Jess looked up puzzled, then dismayed, and hurriedly left the hall. I went after her.

I found her struggling into her coat, cursing her stick and muttering "What on earth possessed you woman."

She glared at me as I took the stick. I said "I thought *I* was the inadequate one."

She went on fighting her coat for a moment, then stopped. The glare gave way to astonishment. "*You?*"

We stood looking at each other. It seemed like a long time. I began to think of some of the ways phrases or gestures can be misinterpreted, multiplying over the years.

Tentatively I held out an arm. "Start again?" I said. "Perhaps I could help with the exhibition?"

For a brief moment Jess looked cautious. Then she took my arm and "Mm, you probably could," she said.

I thought she would quietly forget the idea, but she didn't. I became part of the Committee, mainly fetching and carrying for Jess and Anne. James was delighted with us, especially when the local paper and TV station got interested. So as the millennium date approaches. I am in and out of Manorfields with increasing regularity. Even the twins have been co-opted, along with their school mates and friends in the Guides and Scouts.

RELUCTANT HERO

From the check-out next to Cindy's a stage whisper announced "Here he comes, your weekly boy friend!"

Cindy tossed her head of short dark hair, briefly disturbing the pink streak. But her expression softened. You could set your watch by him each Thursday evening at 6.15. Glancing across to the nearest aisle, between the breakfast cereals and the biscuits, she saw the tall familiar figure: not quite as straight-backed as when she had first noticed him six months ago, though she still always thought of him as a military gentleman. And there was now a special reason for hoping she was right.

That first time, and ever since, he'd had two basket-loads.   She was poised between checking through the streaky bacon and a banana yogurt when her scanner went on the blink.

"It could take a while sir," Cindy had said. "If you'd sooner switch to another check-out..."

He grunted "I'm in no hurry."

She noticed the slightly worn cuffs, the neat darn in his jacket.   Never good at silences she commented "I'd have thought you'd be better with a trolley than two baskets."

"Oh, would you?"

She went on "In fact Thursday evening is one of our busiest times. The mornings are best, early in the week."

After the smallest pause he said tartly "Do you always shower your customers with unwanted advice young lady?" and she'd felt herself go scarlet. Not a thing Cindy was prone to do, nor stammer as she did then "S-sorry s-sir. Gran's always on about my b-bossiness. So's my boyfriend Jason."

Unexpectedly he'd burst out laughing and agreed "Men don't take kindly to it," adding "But actually your concern is quite refreshing in today's indifferent world."

After that Robert Sinclair came to her check-out every Thursday, always with two basket-loads and a mischievous twinkle in his eye. He was also shopping for a friend, liked to keep it separate, he eventually explained. She had gleaned his name and address - Manorfields Care Home, Donnington - from the pension book he dropped one evening. The friend was a fellow resident and as they had full board, he only came in for a few treats: savoury crisps and a few bananas for himself, chocolate biscuits and Imperial mints for the friend. Few enough items, but he liked to keep them separate.

There was rarely much time for a chat but Mr Robert, as Cindy now thought of him, always asked after Gran and sometimes about Jason. She told him how Jason was general dogsbody on the local paper though *she* thought he should be on a college course, adding with a grin "OK, so men don't like bossy women."

Occasionally she wondered about him. One Sunday a trip out on Jason's motorbike brought them through Donnington village. "Stop!" she yelled in his ear as they came to a large house on the outskirts with a sign which read "Manorfields Care Home." She peered over the hedge and saw it was one of those old country-house conversions but noticed there were extensive grounds with a scattering of smaller buildings which might be flats or bungalows.

In answer to Jason's "So what goes on here?" Cindy explained "It's where one of my regulars, Mr Sinclair, lives. Like clockwork he comes, every Thursday evening, 6.15."

"Picking up old men now, eh?" Jason said. "Come here and give us a kiss."

And then his paper began a special series headed *Where are they now?* Everybody was doing stuff on the anniversary of the First World War, but Jason's boss suddenly had this fixation on World War Two as well. "Reckon it's his way of drumming up readership," Jason said. "A good dose of nostalgia - the oldies love it."

The idea was to trace all sorts of people who had lived in the area and made their mark one way or another in the last hundred years. They published photographs of them from the archives urging readers to help in finding out if any were still living locally; among them were several who had distinguished themselves in some way in the Second World War.

"Can't see the point myself," Jason said. "I mean it's history, isn't it?"

But Cindy was fascinated by old films and the stories Gran had told her, especially of those war days. Then her pulse quickened one day as, among the published archive pictures, she noticed one of a clean shaven young man with the neat short-back-and-sides of the time; and the name under it: Zapper Sinclair.

The text below described how Flight Lt R.E.Sinclair DFC, known as Zapper to his comrades, had won great distinction during the famous Battle of Britain. Later he'd been grounded after multiple wounds received in combat.

Jason peered over her shoulder. "Hey wasn't Sinclair the name of that old boyfriend of yours?"

"Don't be so daft," Cindy said, only later wondering why she felt the need to protect her Mr Robert from the lovable but not exactly over-sensitive man in her life.

Now as Robert Sinclair methodically arranged his purchases on the moving belt of Cindy's check-out she looked at him with new interest. He didn't look a war hero but then what did a war hero look like over 50 years on? She'd put a copy of the local paper by the till.

"That's the rag my Jason works for."

"I'm afraid we don't get it out where I live."

Cindy slid it into his carrier bag. "Have a read."

But in answer to her "What did you think of it?" the following Thursday he merely said "An excellent training ground I would imagine."

And that's how things might have stayed, only very soon after Jason said more insistently "I suppose that old boyfriend of yours must have been in the war."

Surprised Cindy said "Why?"

He shrugged. "Our photo call's been running out of steam and the boss has got dead keen on this local hero lark. I told you - it's all about boosting circulation among the wrinklies. He's aiming for a new series in the New Year. I could do with impressing him. How about I come 'n ask the old boy?"

Cindy said quickly "He's more likely to talk to me."

But it was already the beginning of December and time was running out. In a burst of festive indulgence the supermarket management festooned tinsel along the display shelves and dispensed wall-to-wall seasonal muzak. Cindy noticed Mr Robert had added the odd box of chocolates or jar of bath foam to his weekly shop and tried to guess whom they were for.

One or two of the carers perhaps? Or a visiting great niece? Somehow she didn't think of him as married with a family of his own. And then what about the lady he did the shopping for, because by now Cindy was determined there had to be a gentle romance in her Mr Robert's life.

Once she nearly reminded him about getting some Christmas wrapping paper and then thought better of it. Just as well because the following week there it was, balanced across one of his baskets: deep red with green sprigs of holly on it. .

Cindy said approvingly "I see you're well set up for Christmas."

Uncharacteristically Mr Robert looked quite enthusiastic. "An old friend is coming; we haven't met for more years ..." He stopped and smiled "Certainly more years than you can count birthdays for."

Here was her chance. Cindy took a deep breath as she deftly dealt with the contents of his two baskets. "Yeah, I guess it's a time for looking back, isn't it? - Christmas and the New Year."

Mr Robert went on looking at her, still smiling. "My dear," he said, "The most remarkable thing about another new year is that I have lived to see it!" And Cindy knew that, in the gentlest possible way, she had been told to mind her own business.

But it would have been useless telling that to Jason.

That last Thursday before Christmas everything happened so quickly it was only later that Cindy was able to get it in some kind of order. She remembered feeling very tired and thinking she never, ever, wanted to hear *Jingle Bells* again. She noticed Mr Robert and his two baskets at almost exactly the same moment she saw Jason come into the store.

Then she saw Mr Robert stumble and crash to the ground. She hurtled out of her check-out to help him and saw Jason vault over an empty counter to join her. She heard Mr Robert say faintly but firmly "Just give me a moment young lady; nothing hurt except my pride," and immediately after Jason's "Excuse me - Mr Sinclair, isn't it? Flight Lieutenant Zapper Sinclair?"

She heard herself say "It's not him you moron. Push off Jason" even as she knew beyond doubt from Mr Robert's expression and the massive scarring revealed by his pushed-up trouser leg that Zapper Sinclair this certainly was.

A store supervisor helped him to a seat by the check-out while Cindy gathered up his scattered belongings. Meeting his eye she recognised that he knew that she knew - and that what he wanted more than anything else in the world was to leave the past untouched in the privacy of his memory.

She took his hand briefly. "Maybe now you'll use a trolley," she said, then almost without thinking, "Perhaps I could come and see you some time. I'd like to know more about that war."

He grunted "Bossy woman," then gave a small smile. "Yes, I'd like that. Bring your boy friend." He fished in his pocket, brought out a card and handed it to her. "That's the address. Now, you'd better go and make it up with him."

LASTING WAVES

"Letter for you, Bee," Annie poked her head round the door waving a rectangular envelope bearing interesting-looking stamps. "From Oz," she added. "You have a daughter there don't you?"

"Mm." Bee took the envelope and examined it and said, "But that's not Laura's writing. Wonder who it's from"

"Only one way to find out," Annie's fading voice said as she hurried on with further deliveries.

Bee opened it carefully. The writing covering several pages remained unfamiliar. She skimmed through to the end. It ended *so I'll be back in Blighty in a few weeks' time and thought I might look you up.* It was signed *Oddie* and then in brackets, very neatly, *Jeremy Strange.* And in a moment Bee was back nearly twenty years.

----oOo----

All the world had seemed on the move in Terminal Three at London Airport that April morning nearly twenty years ago. Security-checked, Bee Carruthers found a seat within easy glance of the flickering departures screen and kept an eye on Flight BZ 398 to Kuala Lumpur and Perth. Perth, Australia, that is.

It had seemed a great idea in the first flush of euphoria after winning that prize. A new life, she'd thought. Everyone had kept telling her she should move on. Not exactly start again. Well, hardly. Not on just the wrong side of fifty. But Laura, their youngest, had been on at her for months, almost since Robin died.

"The twins would be so chuffed," she emailed and repeated over the phone. "And it would be such a help now I've started that course at UWA."

UWA, University of Western Australia. They had planned, she and Robin, to go and visit Perth next year. There had even been talk of taking early retirement and maybe, just maybe, emigrating. Then the young policewoman had arrived to tell her that Robin had died on the train from London. A massive coronary. It had been days before she could cry, two years before she stopped unexpectedly bursting into tears, and the dominating thought, round and round and round in her head, was "*but he didn't say goodbye*".

"Excuse me." Bee jerked back to the here-and-now of Terminal Three to face a middle-aged woman close to tears. "This must sound kinda crazy, but I've lost my husband."

Bee bit back "So have I" because it was clearly not the sense in which the poor woman meant it, and said instead "The usual meeting place is over there. By Information. See?" Already a lanky figure loping from that direction was calling "Hon! Hi, Hon!" and they hurried into each other's arms. The woman turned to give her a grateful smile and Bee felt momentarily bereft as they disappeared into the crowd. Briefly it had felt involving to the exclusion of all else to be part of someone else's story.

Soon the departures screen was urging her to Gate 55. Half a mile of corridors and moving walkways later, she presented her boarding card and passport. Another waiting lounge, but smaller this time. Bee surveyed the motley collection of humanity with whom she would be sharing the same space for the next twenty-something hours, wondering which of them would become her neighbour. She still felt guilty that she had splashed out on a Business Class ticket, but the prize money for her winning essay had been a surprisingly tidy sum. "For heaven's sake Mother," Laura had said. "What do you think Dad would have wanted?" Of course she was right. "Go for it, lover," he would have said with that grin, part tender, part teasing, that she still missed so abominably.

There were a lot of young families, a large group of bush-hat wearing youngsters who certainly would not be throwing their money around. Others were less easy to categorise. Oh well, she'd find out soon enough.

Half an hour later, as she arranged the cushion in her back, slid her book into the pocket in the back of the seat in front, adjusted her seat belt, a young man nodded at her and settled in the next seat. He had a laptop and looked unobtrusive. Anyway, there seemed acres of space compared with her previous flights, economy of course, to self-catering holidays in various parts of the Mediterranean. Oh, and a couple of business trips with Robin as his marketing enterprise expanded into Europe. One in particular came to mind – a conference in Rome – and it must have lodged there for a while, for she was abruptly aware of that slight physical jolt as of letting go as the aircraft lost contact with the ground. There was a brief swirling of grey as they rose through cloud, and then they were out and up into the sunshine, small patchworks of green between the clouds far, far below. Bee felt herself relax.

Her companion had already got his laptop open and was tapping at his keyboard. She gave him a quick look. Neat haircut, no sign of designer stubble, almost old-fashioned in appearance. And yet something about him was reminiscent of her Jed who had brought her to the airport. Of the three kids, Robin had always said

Jed, their second, would be the single-minded one. Always was a good judge of character. No, not was. Had been. Never would be again. Bee felt herself hurtling back to the edge of the abyss that became synonymous with life the day she opened the door to the young policewoman.

"Stop it!" Bee said sharply.

"Sorry?" Fingers paused in their tapping and a pair of brown eyes surveyed her questioningly.

"No, *I'm* sorry." Bee shook her head apologetically. "Must have dozed off. I'm Bee Carruthers by the way."

"As in busy?" The young man smiled. It was a nice smile.

"Pardon?"

"Bee as in busy? I have this awful habit of word association. Probably too much computing."

She smiled back. "It's short for Beatrice."

"I'm Jeremy Strange."

"Now, that *is* strange. My son is Jeremy though he will insist on shortening it to Jed."

A wry grimace. "My bosses would throw a major wobbly if I did such a thing – well you might guess from *their* names – Good, Strange and Pritchett."

"They do sound rather conservative."

"Mm. So what does your Jed do?"

"Primarily he's into saving the world, but in between he helps his partner Mel run a pre-school group. Catch 'em young is his motto." Suddenly Bee had a memory of opening the door to an unexpected and uncharacteristically troubled Mel. The gist of it was that she wanted a baby, and Jed thought it was too soon. You're only twenty-five Bee had pointed out. She wanted children while she was young enough to continue growing up with them, Mel said. Bee had never seen her so definite, stubborn. She thought the word marriage even came into the conversation. Marriage, it seemed, was becoming fashionable again. Anyway, Mel went on, what was the point of saving the world if there was no one to save it for. It hadn't been the moment to point out this was an argument riddled with more holes than substance.

Jeremy Strange was still looking at her. She said "Sorry, don't let me interrupt your work. I promise not to be a garrulous old woman."

He began to say something, changed his mind, returned to his keyboard. Bee watched him, admiring his dexterity. Her own modest computing skills were restricted to emails and reports for a local conservation group for which she had recently been gently bullied into being the secretary.

After a while she turned her attention to the panel of controls in her arm rest, giving her access to a barrage of entertainment programmes on the screen in front of her. She scrolled through them, came to rest on the screen of flight information: altitude, 10,600 metres; ground speed, 743 kph; temperature outside, minus 47 degrees C; distance to destination ….

She must have slept for she was next aware of the steward leaning across to set up the folding table over her knees. She stretched herself awake, glanced at her watch, could hardly credit that two hours had passed. Jeremy Strange was watching a film.

"Any good?" she asked.

He shrugged. "A predictable romance, but it passes the time."

Bee found herself wondering whether he had any romance in his life. "So what do Messrs. Good, Strange and Pritchett do? Are they as imposing as they sound?"

"Small firm of solicitors. Country town. But very successful."

"And you are the Strange?"

"My stepfather."

She made an apologetic face. "I'm being outrageously nosey – not usually one of my more glaring faults. It must be the effect of this weird limbo of trans-Continental flying."

He nodded. "Ships that pass in the night – not leaving lasting waves." After a moment he added "I was known as Oddie at achool."

"Oddie? Oh yes. Oddie – Oddball – Strange."

"I see you're into word association, too. Are you a writer?"

"Good Lord, no. Just a Mum, Grandmum." She didn't mean to add "Widow."

"Oh, I'm so sorry."

She gave a small shrug. "There are a lot of us about, though not all with the benefit of thirty-two richly happy years. It was a heart attack. No time for goodbyes. But a great legacy. Robin believed totally that you should always follow your star and encouraged the children to do just that. It made for some tempestuous teenage years, but they all know exactly where they are going."

Jeremy Strange said, "Lucky them. My Dad died when I was nine. He didn't say goodbye either." Abruptly he began fiddling with the cutlery on his tray. "How about a more cheerful topic. Like why you're going to Oz? I assume you are going all the way?"

"Oh yes. I'm afraid I had to look up Kuala Lumpur on the atlas when I saw we were landing there. As for reasons, my youngest, Laura, is in Perth. Nice husband, nice two kids. Just about to start a Human Resources course at University."

"And hoping Grannie might be able to help out?" He turned to look at her and added quite seriously "I must say you don't *look* like a Grannie."

"Thanks. I think your assessment is about right. But I'm not sure I'm quite ready to swap my bit of the globe. How about you?"

"Probably doing precisely that. It depends on this particular mission. Amazingly Good, Strange and Pritchett are thinking of opening an Antipodean office. So many of our clients over the years have retired to Oz – you know, to be near their kids; or maybe even doing a bit of late adventuring themselves. This is by way of an exploratory trip."

"Well, you'll certainly be able to call yourself Jed there. I gather the Aussies don't know the meaning of standing on ceremony." He grinned. It made him look younger, more like her Jed. "And since we're into outrageous curiosity, do tell me that a nice young man like you has an appropriately nice young woman waiting for him."

"Did have. A brilliant graphic designer. We were together five – no, six years. Gave each other plenty of space."

"How interesting." He glanced at her sideways to see if she were being ironic. But she wasn't. The idea of giving or being given space was totally novel. She never remembered having any that wasn't filled with the next pile of ironing, meal, school run, extra-curriculum activity, shopping expedition, PTA meeting. Even though Robin had more than pulled his weight.

"You're probably right," Jeremy said, though Bee had made no further comment. "So much space that we ended up losing each other in it." He sounded sad but not heartbroken.

The steward removed their trays, brought them a nightcap. Jeremy opted for a Scotch, Bee for a brandy. She scrolled through the entertainments programmes again and came to rest on a map of the world across which an image of an aeroplane moved imperceptibly. The world map gradually contracted as they zoomed in to ever smaller areas encompassed by the darkness below. It was like a map of 20th century history, she thought: the old Habsburg and Ottoman empires, the stricken Middle East, India once the jewel in the Empire's crown, Korea, Vietnam. It was Robin who had given her a sense of history. Suddenly she felt bone-marrow weary. She found the controls to tip back her seat and hardly had time to wonder at the unexpected comfort before she was asleep.

----oOo----

She awoke five hours later to a new brightness of lights and an announcement that breakfast would be served before their arrival in Kuala Lumpur. Jeremy was busy at his laptop again.

Bee stayed with her thoughts. Early morning hours were still her worst time when a Robin-less future took a vice-grip on her stomach and her mind was knotted with anxiety.

"Good night?" Jeremy enquired as a breakfast tray banished his laptop.

"Surprisingly. I hope you weren't working all through it."

"Something you said set me thinking."

"Good heavens! Tell me more."

"I'll do better and show you in due course." Jeremy said and refused to be drawn further.

Below, there was an impression of palm trees, shaggy vegetation, the slender pointing fingers of minarets as they lost height. The Club lounge at Kuala

Lumpur airport had enormous windows overlooking the main concourse. Jeremy had got there ahead of her and made a beeline for the computer room. Bee felt a twinge of disappointment. In the early daylight of this strange environment, she felt the need for reassurance, even the reassurance of such a new acquaintance.

She poured herself a coffee and sat beneath a huge television screen silently imparting news. It looked no less violent for being soundless.

And then Jeremy was at her side. "Now I'll show you what I meant," he said and led her to one of a battery of computers in a little room off the lounge. The screen was full of doodles which, on closer examination, proved to be animated creatures: animals or beings that you could not quite put a name to, but felt might come to life at any moment. You could imagine them interacting, creating worlds and adventures. Jeremy moved the mouse to scroll through an ever expanding population.

"They're delicious!" Bee exclaimed because she could think of no other word. "I want that one (an almost-chipmunk) and that one (a nearly-frog) and …" She wasgenuinely enchanted.

Jeremy laughed, pleased. "They are my own personal menagerie. Quite a few date from the middle of last night. It was what you said – or your husband said, about following your star. It was like a curtain lifting, and there were all these characters waiting in the wings."

"You mean they're yours – you created them?" Bee said amazed, and when he nodded, "What on earth are you doing being a solicitor?"

"Earning a living. This is just fun."

"Fun, my foot." Bee turned on him severely. "Believe me if my arty daughter, Karen, saw these, she would be talking TV cartoons, book illustrations, product designs...." Karen had just started her own company, putting her all into it as she did with everything.

"Have you any more children up your sleeve?"

"Three's enough, thank you." They'd tried so very hard to keep her busily occupied: Karen with action-packed trips to London; Jed and Mel with country expeditions; Laura with daily calls. She was incredibly lucky.

Then she saw Jeremy's expression. He said "Dad was an artist. My early childhood was alive with his drawings. We never had any money, but it was all such *fun*. Not sure Mother thought so. Anyway when she married Step-papa it was like moving from an adventure playground to a disciplined classroom."

"Does it have to be a life sentence?"

He didn't answer immediately. Then, "Glad you like them. I think we're about due to board again."

----oOo----

Still a few hours to go. How odd that one could become so attached to detachment that there was something scary about the prospect that it was about to end. And yet re-attachment would mean reunion with her lovely Laura and family, whom Bee had barely had a chance to get to know.

"Perhaps you could come over and meet the family in Perth," she found herself saying.

"I wish." Jeremy sounded genuinely regretful. "But I've only a couple of nights before I move on to Sydney." He had never actually specified where his new office might be. Bee felt absurdly disappointed.

"By the way," he added. "How will your Jed and Karen manage if you move to Australia?"

She hadn't really thought about it. "I don't think they need me. Not in that sense."

Well, there was that uncharacteristic tension between Jed and Mel about babies. And Karen's single minded dedication to her new enterprise had been the death knell to her first long term relationship. But they weren't the sort of things she could advise on. Were they?

Jeremy said, "Have you asked them?"

"No."

"Don't you think you should?" He glanced at her slyly. "You could tell Karen about my website, if you really think she'd be interested."

Lunch came and went. Odd dots of land far, far below presaged a vast continent. And then the continent itself, unimaginable acres stretching to the horizon and no doubt to many horizons beyond that. It swirled in swathes of terracotta stippled with green, a dried-up river bed snaking through it. Not a sign of life as she knew it. She found herself imagining it through the eyes of the first settlers. How could they have found the courage – not just the courage, but the imagination to visualise all the potential that had turned this barren land into a leader of the modern world? It had to be a young person's country.

She must have spoken aloud for Jeremy said "I don't think so. As I told you, a lot of our retired clients have emigrated here. They all seem as happy as sandboys and girls."

Laura had said as much, quoting a whole range of societies involved in the kind of activities that appealed to Bee: gardening, quilting, choral music. "You could rent the house. Try it for a year."

It all sounded so reasonable. If only Robin were here…. Her throat tightened. Well, he wasn't. She had to make her own decisions.

Yes, her *own* decisions.

Not Laura's, or Jed's, or Karen's.

And suddenly Bee knew just what she wanted to do. Following your star was one thing, but first you had to know your star. "Write down that website of yours," she said. "And I'll pass it on to Karen when I get home." She noted his raised eyebrows. "You're right. Needs more thought, more consultation. And after this visit I'll have a better idea, won't I?"

"You will," Jeremy said, seriously.

"And so will you."

A short pause, then "I'm beginning to think some passing ships leave quite lasting waves."

He smiled, nodded. "I reckon you're right," he said.

Bee had stayed three months in Perth before deciding, kind as everyone was, she was too much a European at heart to make the final move. She was surprised at how delighted Jed, Mel and Karen had been to have her back. Also surprising was the fact that Jeremy Strange had been in touch with Karen who, as Bee forecast, had completely fallen for his 'population'. Karen had put him in touch with a rising young author and a series of children's books was in the offing. Jeremy had telephoned to thank her for the contact and, in due course, Karen had presented her with a copy of the first book.

Bee settled in sheltered accommodation in the grounds of Manorfields Care Home an hour or so's drive from Jed and Mel, who in time produced a son and a daughter.

Now, nearly twenty years later, she fingered the envelope that had brought her this link with the past and, for some reason, her last words to Jeremy as they lost height over Australia came to mind: *lasting waves indeed.*

DRIVE CAREFULLY

It's what everyone says, isn't it, when you set off in a car? 'Drive carefully'. Whether it's a few miles to the supermarket or overland to India. It's what I say to my daughter-in-law Becky as she gets into her car after visiting me at Manorfields care home, where I've been for three years. She comes twice most weeks, and once a month takes me out for a country run and a pub lunch. 'Drive carefully' was also what our neighbour said when we dropped in the house keys (she watered our plants) before heading for Turkey.

It was to be our last big trip, so Rex said. He said it every time we plan another big trip so I didn't take too much notice.

"Best go back before the EU ruins it," he said this time.

It looked a very long way on the map. I imagined our ageing campervan inching across it, and thought it was a bit like life: setting out from A and creeping – though in the case of life with ever gathering momentum – towards Z. Of course, who's to know precisely when, or where, Z will be? Judging by statistical averages, we're both, as it were, well-passed Istanbul already.

Rex had always been the route planner. He spread maps all over the dining table for days, working out the best if not the quickest routes. Once he looked up from manoeuvring a way through the industrial Ruhr and grunted "Trouble with getting old is that so many place names resonate. I passed over most of these on those 1000-plane raids of Bomber Harris."

"Perhaps better not mention that if we're camping in the area."

"Hmmm." He gave me one of those grins which took 50 or so years off his four-score and five: the grin of a small boy caught in some mildly wicked act, or of a deeply familiar friend complicit in some shared experience.

He was also ace at packing the camper van so I left him to that, too. It involved elaborate lists, much muttering under breath and innumerable to-ings and fro-ings between house and car port. Plastic containers of all sizes and shapes crowded every surface of the kitchen for days as dry goods were stored, labels applied, and boxes acquired from the local co-op, the measurements of each appropriate to the space it would occupy. My task was to keep track of what was in each container, box and space, but given the number of changes that occurred in the packing process, this aim was quite unrealistic.

I was also the one who did the paperwork, relentlessly pursuing every scrap – tickets, insurance certificates, lists of camp sites, road tunnels, toll charges, traffic regulations for a dozen countries – that was briefly borrowed as 'just want to check something; do stop fussing, woman'. I did the note for the milkman, for the plant-watering neighbour, the post office for holding our mail, the gardener, and notified all persons likely to try and contact us while we were away. It took at least the three-four hour drive to the port to stop agonising about what we might have forgotten.

So we set off from A, in this case Harwich, for a millpond crossing to Hook of Holland. Our European Sites guide listed a camp near Arnhem, so we mused over the bridge whose taking cost such a spectacular and largely avoidable sacrifice in 1945. I was at school at the time, but Rex – by then a prisoner-of-war for over two years – was being marched back and forth across a dwindling chunk of Germany. A column parallel to the one he was in got shot up by some of our own Typhoons. Fifty dead. Some of them had been prisoners almost since the beginning of the war and they were then within a month of the end of it. Rex wept when he spoke of it.

Next day we crossed into Germany. I always thought that *ausfahrt,* the German word for a motorway exit, sounded rather rude and tended to distract me from the destinations to which it was *ausfahrt*ing. I was, however, jolted by memory into noticing the *ausfart* to Ingolstadt, north of Munich. Then I was straight back to that steamy July day on the river Danube, me in a kayak on the second day of a course, Rex on the river bank, except I hadn't known he was Rex then. Fast forward to me *in* the Danube under the kayak, and something grabbing and pulling at me as I fought for breath, desperate not to die. On the bank I found myself surveyed by very blue eyes. He was a bit breathless himself, and said "You look like a drowned rat."

I vomited up water. "A nearly drowned rat" I choked. And he grinned that memorable grin at me for the first time. That was fifty-plus years ago.

----oOo----

Autobahn-motorway-autostrade-autoput-driving by whatever name is unspeakably tedious, but in Austria it at least has the compensation of the kind of scenery on which you can refresh your soul. And so into Slovenia, the first of the six republics that had made up the former Yugoslavia before that terrible war, and maybe E on the alphabet of our life's journey to Istanbul.

We'd stayed at the camp site at Bohinjska Bistrica before and the young receptionist, Lisa, remembered. But then Rex was rather unforgettable. She had been a student that last time when Rex re-climbed Triglav, Slovenia's highest mountain, on his 80th birthday. Happily another ascent did not appear to be on his agenda, so we went instead to admire Lisa's chubby new baby and meet her bus driver husband. The house was a traditional Slovene chalet, with wood stacked under the eaves, and tubs overflowing with geraniums and petunias. The garden was a strip of meadow scattered with apple trees and a tethered dun cow grazing. It was one of those countless moments in our travels which affirmed why we continued insatiably to do them, and why we did them together.

The Dalmatian coast had not changed for the better with an ever-lengthening ribbon of *sobe-zimmer*-rooms, *apartmenti*, motels, pensions. I thought back nostalgically to our earliest visits when the Dalmatian *magistrale* was slowly inching its way along that magnificent coastline, turning stony dusty lanes into a sinuous ribbon of tarmac. A Croat friend, who was something in tourism, pointed out the tiny terraced fields, cleared with painstaking dedication, stone by stone removed to create the walls separating one few square metres of field from another: here an olive tree, there a handful of vines.

"The next generation won't bother with this," our friend said. And now it was patently obvious that the next generation hadn't.

"It's called progress," Rex said when I voiced the thought.

"Is it?"

"Well, would you want to break your nails and your back on that soil?" he asked, reasonably enough.

"Those sorts of life styles are mainly romantic to those who don't have to live them."

Below our ribbon of tarmac, crystal clear water shaded from turquoise to purple. We found a camp site in a meadow atop a steep descent to that sea at Mlini, a few miles south of Dubrovnik. Maybe 'H' on our alphabetic journey. We liked it so much we stayed several days, caught up with the laundry, dipped in and out of the sea and, in the family-run restaurant on the shore, nibbled at juicy *raznjići*, the Croatian version of the shish-kebabs that would form our staple diet when we got to Turkey.

Rex was looking younger by the day. A semi-insomniac at home, he sleeps like a babe in the camper van. His ability to relax seemed to be in direct proportion to our increasing distance from the mail and telephone. Especially the telephone. He argued that it is an instrument of the devil and will go to extremes to avoid picking it up.

While we were at Mlini, Rex collected a Swedish couple and a lone birdwatching Dutchman, demonstrating another unfathomability of my unfathomable man. At home he was affectionately known as O.C., acronym for old curmudgeon from his self-professed antipathy to the social round. Yet pop him into a camp site with a load of strangers and in no time he has ferreted out the most interesting.

We usually ended up with a small party, and I loved it as much as he did. In fact, each trip provided an opportunity to renew acquaintance with a Rex who, between times, burrows under protective layers. "Cultivated old-fogeyism," one of our closer friends said and was probably right. I wished it were not so. Our sons rarely saw the real Rex, and it was the discerning middle one, now approaching middle age himself, who glimpsed through the layers and kept in closest touch, his concern expressed in a kind of bantering resignation over what eccentric caper would be the next on his father's expanding repertoire.

"Where have all the donkeys gone?" I mused a few days later.

We had crossed into Bosnia-Hercegovina, which I'd always thought to be one of the more accessible of Europe's few remaining areas of wild magnificence. Rushing green torrents, precipitous gorges, soft uplands studded with wild flowers beneath rocky crags; women, faces lined with an eon of wisdom, spinning wool as they watched their flock; and wide rackety carts drawn by horse, mule or donkey. Now replaced entirely by tractors and clapped-out cars.

The theme for one of those freedom songs had been haunting me for hours. I found myself putting words to it:

> "*Where have all the donkeys gone?*
> *No more trotting.*
> *The tractors in their place*
> *Will never have their grace.*"

Rather pleased with that I started:

"*Where are all the roadside geese?*"
"No more honking," suggested Rex.

"*Now only plastic bags*
Flap in a world of tattered rags." I finished

"Hmmmm. Doesn't quite scan. But not bad, not bad."

It was late afternoon when we reached Mostar, spilling down steep slopes to the Neretva river. There was no camp site so we booked into a pension next to a mosque from whose minaret, at sunrise, the recorded call to prayer gently nudged us into the new day.

The old town was pitted with destruction – burnt-out shells of homes, rubble and rubbish everywhere. Framed by the gaping walls on one building we got our first glimpse of the reconstructed single span bridge built in 1566, destroyed by the Croats in a matter of minutes of mortar fire. The new bridge was a clone of the original, but it looked what it was: spanking shiny new. It had taken its predecessor over four centuries to acquire its patina.

A couple of days later we found that we had the Oaza Camp site at Ilidža, a few km from Sarajevo, to ourselves: a fine grassy meadow with well laid-out trees and a superb shower block that didn't work. I guessed we must be at 'L' or 'M' by now.

Ilidža is a spa where the Archduke Franz Ferdinand spent his last night before reviewing his troops in June 1914 in the capital of the then Austro-Hungarian protectorate of Bosnia. An 18-year-old terrorist/freedom fighter called Gavrilo Princip shot and fatally wounded him, providing one of the triggers for the First World War. Indeed, that 'war to end all wars'. Sarajevo, it seems, had an unfortunate talent for making the world's darker headlines. We took the tram into the city the next morning. There were regiments of high-rise blocks of flats, pitted with black window sockets where yet another mortar had hit and destroyed yet another home during the siege of the 1990s; there were new mosques, their multiple minarets pronouncing the Saudi origins of the aid which had rebuilt them; there was the rebuilt Holiday Inn almost obscene in its shiny gaudiness, long-robed figures sweeping in and out of it. But the older parts of the city were visually pleasingly, as long as you didn't notice the gravestones hurriedly erected, usually in the middle of a mortar raid, wherever there was a space.

Yes, well, the 21st century has produced other terrorists, other freedom fighters.

We were beginning to feel we were in the Balkans now, and the feeling increased as we headed into Serbia. The inconvenience of having to cross borders every hundred miles or two where earlier there had been none triggered unanswerable question as to who had gained, and what, by so much destruction and bloodshed. The border crossings which were relatively straight forward along the coast and across the plains became less obvious among the labyrinth of winding mountain roads. And these Serb-Bosnian borderlands, deeply ravined, thickly wooded, were the same as those which provided shelter and a bloody setting for guerilla warfare in World War Two.

"It must have been around here that I was dropping supplies during the war," Rex observed. "For that Tito fellow. Don't imagine he would have thought much of this new mania for borders."

And the next moment we had crossed yet another one as we drove passed an onslaught of acronyms representing the international presence in Kosovo.

The main highway through Kosovo served what must be Europe's biggest building site, slightly reminiscent of the approaches to any major US city with its gas stations, shopping malls, and barrage of advertising signs. It all seemed a far cry from the smoke-darkened ancient monasteries we had visited years ago peppering the valleys and mountains within a 50-mile radius: relics of Serbia's medieval empire, wrested from them by the Ottoman Turks following the seminal battle on those very fields of Kosovo in 1389.

Before long we were crossing into northern Greece. I was beginning to feel twitchy and Rex noticed, but I knew better than to share the A-Z superstition which had seized me, imagining the snort of derision that would greet it.

This late in the season, there was not much delay at the border beyond Alexandroupolis. The landscapes of European Turkey did not differ to any marked degree from those of northern Greece. The main difference was in the gas stations where we were offered small glasses of tea while they filled us up and where I spied a small mosque at the end of the forecourt for those whose visit coincided with one of the times of prayer or a desire to meditate.

When I drew his attention to it, Rex agreed that it was a mightily appropriate facility. The Turks are, in the main, a delightful people in any circumstance other than behind the wheel of a vehicle. They do not seem to have grasped the purpose of a rear view mirror, of indicators, or really any feature of the car except its horn which is in constant use.

"Not many women drivers," I thought aloud.

"Hmmmm," Rex said.

We had agreed that under no circumstance would we drive in Istanbul, had selected a camp site on 'our' side of the city and put our trust in Allah. At least I did on behalf of both of us for Rex's relationship with his Maker is tenuous to the point of non-existence. When we eventually found it, it was one of the worst camp sites we had come across. A disconsolate Frenchman was standing guard outside the Gents' showers while his wife splashed away behind an unlockable door. "The water it is salt, of the sea, and only for the *Messieurs* is it heated," he explained.

So had we reached 'Z', I wondered? Was this it? But it didn't really feel like the end of everything or, indeed, anything.

Istanbul was hectic in a loud, colourful, human way; culturally dazzling; and tiring.

"Let's go clockwise," Rex said, meaning directionally round the country, and I felt absurdly safer once we'd crossed the Bosphorus and left the outskirts of the city well behind us.

We barely heard a European language along the north coast which, in all honesty, we didn't find terribly attractive. Having made the grave error in some inland village of succumbing to home-made ice cream, it didn't help that we were both afflicted by violent diarrhoea and holed up for some days in a Black Sea-side camp site.

Once he started feeling better, Rex began plunging down memory lane, something that he was doing more and more. At one time he never mentioned the war and only referred to the scenes of his more colourful escapades when they were mentioned in the news or some documentary, usually to pronounce they did not know what they were talking about. The soul survivor of an avalanche in Nepal, scooped off the Greenland ice cap in the nick of time, precipitated into an Antarctic crevasse, he had had a worrying number of near misses and I couldn't help feeling he was not due for many more.

Now, though, his reminiscences were geographically more immediate. Forty years ago he had climbed a Turkish mountain, befriended a family who lived in a mud-brick hut whose son had been their donkey boy, helping them to carry their equipment to establish a base camp.

"I'd like to go and see what's happened to Ali," he said.

Ali and the relevant mountain were still some distance away in south central Anatolia. I thought this heartland of some of our earliest cultures was one of the dustiest places I'd ever seen. Then we reached the little road, blessedly wooded, that led into the Aladaglar mountain range. Rex had a photograph of the donkey boy, his family, and their mud-brick hut, with the hulk of Demirkazik soaring up behind it. In one of those coincidences that makes life so much stranger than fiction, we showed the photograph to a young man in a small village at the end of a road. He became very excited. "That is my father, and there is my grandfather," he shouted. "Follow me!"

The grandfather had died. But the father Ali, one-time donkey boy, duly arrived and burst into tears when he saw Rex, remembering everything about his earlier visit, even the colour of the car in which they travelled. He had progressed from the one-room hut to an attractive pension he now ran for the trekkers who came here to walk and birdwatch. His son helped when he was on holiday from university and now cooked us an excellent meal of local river fish.

It was difficult to get away. Ali wanted us to go with him to the coast to see his kid sister Fatima, now mother of three, whom Rex had last seen posing on his car bonnet aged four. But we'd lost too much time with our sick stomachs and had to get on. We hit the south coast near the Mediterranean port of Silifka and spent a couple of nights in a pension. Rex said we were going 'soft' but the fact was that camp sites are extremely thin on the ground in 'off-beat' Turkey, and in the more well trodden areas most of them have been covered by high rise hotels or self catering flats. We liked Silifka. It had some very good restaurants where we spent the evening watching the evening ferry load up for its regular connection to Turkish Cyprus, a reminder of one long-running European sore that still needed healing.

As we progressed westwards, Rex became increasingly depressed. Upon his long cherished memories of deserted beaches on which he had spread his sleeping bag to sleep in the open forty years ago was now superimposed the reality of miles of high-rise 'tourist nonsense'. We scuttled through Alanya and Antalya as fast as possible.

Worse was to come at Altinkum, with its wall to wall hotels, pensions, restaurants, souvenir shops, tattoo parlours. Altinkum (justifiably meaning 'golden sands') is one of a scattering of popular south-west Turkey resorts, each dedicated to the every need of a particular visiting nationality. In this case, the Brits were the chosen people. All signs were in English, all prices in Sterling. Menus blared out *Full English Breakfast, Roast Beef and Yorkshire Pudding, Bacon Butties.*

We went for a stroll. The fine sandy beach was crowded with our compatriots of all ages, shapes and sizes wearing the minimum. Mountains of reddening flesh bulged from bikini tops and bottoms, paunchy overhangs wobbled over swimming trunks. Not a pretty sight. In a cyber café where I went to check our email, the youngish owner showed me to a computer, put his hands on my shoulders.

"You like massage?" he asked. "In your dreams," I said and he seemed to get the message. Rex roared with laughter when I reported this.

We escaped to some of the world's greatest archaeological sites, which were numerous and extensive enough to dilute our fellow tourists into acceptable proportions. Ephesus, Pergamon, Troy – you could become dizzy with the resonance of such quantities of history and human experience. Suddenly Rex had had enough. "Let's miss out Istanbul on the way back and side-track through Gallipoli."

I thought of my A-Z. We'd seemingly sailed through the alphabet unscathed. Superstitiously it seemed a good idea not to tempt fate. "Fine by me," I said.

Our visit coincided with howling gales, plummeting temperatures and coach-loads of schoolchildren being taught the importance of this seminal battle to the birth of modern Turkey. At the museum they were more interested in us than in the exhibits.

"They think you're a Gallipoli veteran," I whispered.

Rex was delighted and posed happily with them as they took each other's photographs. Such battalions and freshness of youth made a poignant contrast as we looked down on Anzac and other coves where boys not much older than those youngsters had made the ultimate sacrifice.

By the time we reached Edirne near the Bulgarian border, I reckoned we were going through the alphabet for the second time. Edirne's Selimye Camii Mosque was designed by the same architect as that of Aya Sofya in Istanbul, and I thought it was the most beautiful in Turkey. And a good place to hear the call to prayer for the last time. "I shall quite miss that," Rex said. "Especially the dawn one. It kind of makes a reassuring start to the day."

It was out of earshot that last morning. We were only a few miles from the Bulgarian border when Rex said "Well, we made it." Had he been harbouring his own superstitions? I opened my mouth to say "Don't tempt Providence," when an oncoming car came out of nowhere round a bend and on the wrong side of the road. Our side.

I didn't hear the crash and the blackness which followed gave way only gradually to flickers of greyness peopled by white shadowy figures talking in an incomprehensible language.

"Speak English," I tried to say crossly, but my tongue was too thick to form the words.

"Ah, you're awake," said a voice sounding like Stephen Fry, though its owner looked the archetypical man from the Embassy. His expression was sad and gentle, and I think I knew, as it were, before I knew.

"Rex," I said.

'Stephen Fry' consulted someone behind him, and there was some shuffling about while a wheelchair was found and I was transferred into it. Someone wheeled me through corridors. Painful. The pain helped to concentrate my mind.

Rex was in a little room by himself. He looked like a monstrous mummy punctured by an intricate network of tubes, but his face was unmarked and uncovered and his blue eyes open. He looked quite peaceful and smiled that smile that had captured me half a century earlier.

"The boys are on their way. They will look after you," he said.

It was too early for grief, but I thanked God he had thought of summoning the boys.

He went on, "I have always loved you."

"I know," I said. "And I've always loved you."

"Hmmmmm," Rex said, before he closed his blue eyes and moved gently on to wait for me in wherever there is beyond the dark.

"Drive carefully," I said in my head.

----oOo----

It's not true that it takes two years to recover from bereavement. I suspect it takes forever. But the sharpness of the loss loses its edge and, proportionately, the meaning of the memories gains in reality. The smallest thing can trigger them. In my worst moments I have asked myself whether I would sacrifice them to be free of grief. And, of course, the answer is 'no'. So I just go on telling him to 'drive carefully' wherever he is until I get around to being there to help with the navigation.

MISERERE NOBIS

About six months after she moved to Manorfields Care Home, Evelyn started going to the concerts held regularly at the Parish Church. It took her that long to even begin to feel she could call the village of Donnington home, sell her house, dispose of most of her possessions and turn one room at Manorfields into the semblance of a nest. The staff there were marvellous, but ... Well, the fact was that she still missed John desperately and didn't really feel like being sociable.

It was Siobhan, Freshfield's feisty manager, who suggested she should go out more. "After all," she said, "you're more mobile than most." Evelyn thought it was intended to sound slightly reprimanding.

----oOo----

Et in terra pax hominibus bonae voluntatis. And on earth peace, goodwill towards men.

Evelyn found herself mouthing the words as she followed them on the programme sheet. How they resonated. How they soared with meaning.

Laudamus te. Benedictimus te. We praise you. We bless you. *Adoramus te. Glorificamus te.* We worship you. We glorify you.

She gave a small sigh that was lost against the swelling voices rising to fill every arch, infiltrate round every curlicue and into the highest nook. She closed her eyes drawing the sound into her head …. and when she opened them, found herself looking across crowded pews, passed the conductor, over the massed choir directly at a man in an orange shirt.

He was centre back: the tallest, the slimmest, the most beautiful. And somewhere in the far recesses of her mind, there was a tremor of memory.

For heavens' sake, seventy-somethings were not supposed to get the hots for young ... younger men in visiting choirs. Anyway he probably swore and shouted at his wife.

Ah, lucky wife.

Et in terra pax …. She watched his mouth shape the words. *Adora-a-ah-mus ... Glorifica-a-ah-mus … Laudamus te. Benidictus te.* A wide mouth with thinnish lips, but not too thin.

In a world in which everyone spoke Latin, how could there be anything but civility and good will. Could you swear in Latin?

You could certainly be violent in Latin. Think of all those wars, and all that decadence. Wasn't it decadence that had finished off invincible Rome in the end?

Well, she wouldn't mind a bit of decadence with that one in the orange shirt. And how would you say that in Latin? She visualised her Latin teacher, who you couldn't imagine being decadent with anyone. "Clearly Evelyn Meredith you have more important things on your mind, but perhaps you would be good enough to translate the passage underlined on page 43." Something about horses and battlefields. Boring, boring, boring.

Why an orange shirt? Most of the others were in white or blue. Perhaps he liked to stand out in a crowd. Evelyn hoped not. She liked to think of him as modest, considerate.

Like John. Only John would never have worn an orange shirt. A thin stripe was his preference, tidy, inspiring confidence as befitted the banking clerk who rose gently through the ranks. They had been so right for each other: she the born nest-builder, he the steady reliable bread-winner. No doubt seeming unbelievably boring in the eyes of the great and the good of the delightful Cotswold village that had become their patch. But they'd had their moments, indeed quite a lot of them. Oh yes.

Even after three years she missed him dreadfully. Especially the wonderful silliness they triggered in each other.

----oOo----

It was Judith who had persuaded her to come to the concert in the parish church: Rossini's *Petite Messe Solennelle*. It would do her good, was the implication, though she didn't suppose drooling over the man in the orange shirt was what Judith had in mind.

People were always trying to do her good; it went with the territory of being widowed, and a bit mousey, and virtually childless with both son and daughter in Australia. And once they'd started, they couldn't seem to stop: wanting her to 'move on', though where to was never made clear. She was forever being asked to make up the numbers at little dinner parties, to go on coach outings, join committees for this or that 'if only you could spare the time'. They did not know, of course, about the Internet module she had enrolled on for Creative Writing, and which took an enormous amount of her time. It felt like the only bit of privacy she had left.

That and her thoughts. Thank God (*miserere nobis*) John had not been excised from her head in the way he had been physically excised from her life. She felt a bubble of laughter rising as she remembered the giggles they'd had over the Creative Writing course decision.   Little Evelyn of the home-made jams and hand-made lampshades on a Creative Writing Course! And, astonishingly, she was proving to be quite good at it.   That's what I call moving on, John had said approvingly.   So what would he think about Orange Shirt?

Don't be stupid, woman.   He probably knew about him before you did.   Remember how often they had thought each others thoughts, simultaneously starting to speak the same words like some Greek chorus.

Qui tollis peccata mundi, miserere nobis – You who take away the sins of the world, have mercy upon us.

How old would Orange Shirt be?   Difficult to tell from this distance.   Anywhere between late-thirties and mid-fifties.   One of those thinnish faces, sensitive but still quite rugged.   Straight nose, highish cheekbones, wide apart eyes, but far too distant to tell the colour.   And tanned as if he spent a lot of time outdoors.   Perhaps he was a gardener.   Or a sports teacher.   Or maybe it came out of a bottle?   Was his hair going a bit thin on top?

It'll be a mixed choir, Judith had said.   The usual lot of our best local talent boosted by Felicitas, a miscellany of semi professionals who lived in the area and got together whenever they could.   They quite often gave concerts, usually for charity, but Evelyn had always managed to wriggle out of it before, salving her conscience with a substantial donation.   This time there could be no excuse; Judith had been there when Evelyn's niece had rung to say she'd got a bug and must cancel her week-end visit.

"So now you can come to the concert," Judith said.   "It will break up the week-end for you."

82

Evelyn had arrived very early and chosen an aisle seat in the back pew. She knew Judith's favourite position was the third pew which she would share with the Featheringtons and the Walkers, and where she would no doubt keep a place for Evelyn.

"No, really," Evelyn said when Judith paused to tell her just that. "I'd rather not be too near the front."

"All right, dear. But you'll join us afterwards, won't you. I'm giving a little soirée? Some of the choir will join us."

Including Orange Shirt?

Cum Sancto Spiritu, in gloria Dei Patris – With the Holy Ghost, in the glory of God the Father. Amen – Amen A-a-a-a-ah-men.

----oOo----

There was a 20-minute interval with wine at £1 a shot, orange juice 50p. Sometimes concert performers would circulate among the audience at this time, but it must have been decided on this occasion that the choir was far too big because they disappeared behind a curtain beyond which they no doubt had their own supplies. Evelyn stayed in her seat.

"Do join us? I believe it's a very good Chilean," Judith paused on her way passed.

It would sound churlish to say their chatter got in the way of the music – and the thoughts of Orange Shirt - still filling her head.

"I think I'll just sit here," Evelyn said meaninglessly, and Judith nodded in apparent understanding.

Did other women of a certain age fantasise in this way? It was a bit like sex when you were young. You couldn't imagine your parents doing it even though you were incontrovertible proof that they had. But she really couldn't imagine that terribly nice old girl (watch it, she's probably not much older than you are) who organised meals-on-wheels lusting over some young Adonis; or that prissy man who edited the community magazine fancying a bimbo.

Hang on, you've no idea what old men fantasise about, John's voice observed in her head, and she smiled in welcome at it.

It coincided with a burst of commotion as people went back to their seats, and the choir filed down the aisle, giving her a first closer view of Orange Shirt. He really was extraordinarily attractive. She felt her cheeks flare as he caught her eye. Could she really have imagined that he winked?

Deum de Deo, lumen de lumini – God of Gods, Light of Light.

I know who he reminds you of, John said.

Whom, corrected Evelyn. And of whom are you speaking.

Of Orange Shirt, dearest Pedant. He reminds you of me.

You?

She must have squeaked aloud for Jocelyn Walters looked round from the pew in front, frowning slightly.

Yes me. Remember that one and only time our youth club had a go at amateur dramatics – some pantomime thing? Though I say it myself, I was quite personable in those days. They cast me as the Prince and put me in those awful tights.

God, yes. Tights weren't in it. When you were drooling over what's-her-name – Audrey something who played the witch-disguised-as-princess, it was positively embarrassing. Never did understand what you saw in her.

That, my sweet, was because I saw absolutely nothing in her at all. As for any embarrassment that was entirely your fault when you suddenly pranced into the rehearsal in that milkmaid outfit.

I didn't realise, Evelyn swallowed another bubble of mirth.

Why do you think I followed you home that evening

Yes, he had, hadn't he.

Et iterum venturus est cum glorium – And he shall come again with glory. *Judicare vivos et mortuos* – to judge both the quick and the dead.

The quick and the dead. Which summed them up to a 't'. John was quiet for a while and Evelyn once again allowed the music to fill her head. She noticed that Orange Shirt had lifted his chin as though addressing his voice to heaven. She wondered if he were pious as well as choral. Neither she nor John had been very pious, though they had been regular churchgoers because … well, because they always had been and neither of them came up with a good reason why they should stop.

You realise, John commented after a while, *that Orange Shirt and any salacious thoughts you may have towards him are entirely creations of your mind.*

Of course, returned Evelyn impatiently. Just as you are.

No, not just as I am. We have a history you and I. Several decades of it. You have photo-albums full to prove it, so it's hardly something you need to create. Though I suspect you may have forgotten some of our ... our more intense moments.

Remind me.

If you need reminding, perhaps they didn't mean the same to you as to me.

85

I'd rather it were you standing up there than Orange Shirt

Hm. Evelyn sensed a pleased look. *But would you feel the same?*

She really didn't know. I'll have to think about it.

Well, let me know when you've decided. He sounded a bit grumpy. *After all you can conjure me up any time.*

Yes, she could, couldn't she.

Agnus Dei, qui tollis peccata mundi: miserere nobis – Oh Lamb of God, who takes away the sins of the world, have mercy on us.

Suddenly Evelyn felt a wave of weariness so intense it seemed to dilute her bones. She didn't feel a bit sinful. Just horrendously lonely.

I'm glad you're there, she told John. But he wasn't. She spent several minutes trying to get him back; or it must have been longer for she was startled by an explosion of applause. It went on for a long time, the choir bowing and bowing. Yes, Orange Shirt *was* thinning a bit on top. Then they disappeared through the curtain behind them, returning again as the applause continued.

Evelyn waited a while before edging out into the exiting throng. John remained stubbornly unavailable, but Judith was waiting for her in the church porch.

"Ah, there you are. Wasn't that sublime? Wine and nibbles at the Lodge – thank heavens for a fine evening and a large garden; most of the choir are coming."

Miserere nobis.

"So sorry Judith," Evelyn said. "I'd completely forgotten I'm seeing a friend."

Raised eyebrows. "At this time of the evening?"

"So sorry, Judith," Evelyn said again. "An old friend passing through. He got in touch this afternoon. A very old friend."

It sounded marginally less odd than saying she had a date with a photo album.

MOVING ON

As always, as soon as Victoria came into the lounge of Manorfields Care Home, she headed for the television control like a homing pigeon and in seconds they were all being treated to yet another antique show: at full volume. Why wouldn't the woman wear a hearing aid and do them all a favour? In due course one of the carers would come in and turn it down or off, but not before irritation had done negative things to Alison's blood pressure.

She glanced across the room, caught her husband's eye, winked and jerked her head sideways. In a simultaneous move they rose from their seats and headed across the hall, through the dining room to the conservatory beyond. *We're incredibly lucky*, she thought. She meant lucky to be so mobile, so intuitive, so in accord and, above all, together. They were the exceptions in Manorfields, and it could so easily have been otherwise.

For the moment the conservatory was empty and redolent with perfume and colour provided by the lady who came daily to do the flower arrangements. Alison settled herself into an armchair beside an amazing combination of multi-coloured tulips and yellow chrysanthemums and allowed herself, as she quite often did, the luxury of looking back. OK, some people might regard it as romantic women's magazine stuff, but it was her life and it could have been horribly different.

----oOo---

It was thirty years ago and she'd been in the kitchen cutting up peppers for a *ratatouille* when the doorbell rang. It was a few weeks after she had been dumped and culinary work was proving one of the better therapies.

"Sugar," she'd muttered, followed by a silent monologue. *If only they would leave me alone. It's got to the point where I hardly dare leave the cottage for fear of bumping into Jill ('how about a coffee and a chinwag?') or Georgina (' have you thought some more about joining our reading group?)* The associated '*it will help take your mind off things*' was never stated but patently implied.

Damn Darrell.

From the end of the hall she could see the frosted glass over the top of the front door. Well, it was a male-shaped head, so that was a blessing. The head disappeared as the letterbox was pushed open and a voice said, "You there, Alison? This won't take long."

It was Sim Johnson who did the computer courses at the library. "Hang on, just washing my hands," she called and went to turn the taps on in the kitchen.

Sim had been looking after a terminally ill partner before she died a few weeks ago. Alison had noticed them soon after they moved into the village a year or so earlier. Well, it was difficult to miss them. Amanda was already in a wheelchair and Sim was always at her side. Otherwise they kept themselves pretty much to themselves. Sim was a big, broad man, and Alison had been struck by his gentleness.

In those days she had been very much part of the social scene herself, and they had all speculated about his job.

"Builder?" Jill suggested.

"Handyman," offered Georgina. "I could do with someone to put up a shed." Georgina could always do with someone to put up or pull down something

It turned out he was a computer wizard, mostly working from home, designing websites. Then he began Computing-for-the-Terrified classes in the library. Alison, though not terrified, had gone to a few to polish up on desktop publishing. Darrell had fancied himself as a computer nerd but was too impatient as a teacher. Sim, on the other hand, was very patient and Alison looked forward to the lessons. She missed them when Amanda's condition deteriorated and Sim stopped the classes.

By then she and Darrell were an item, the sort that she had truly thought would remain an item forever. Yes, she knew he was married, but he had totally convinced her that it had gone wrong for both of them ages before. Shelagh, his wife, ran a small art gallery in an up-and-coming part of London. She had a partner whom Darrell suspected did not limit his affairs to the business variety.

Though they had never put it into so many words, Alison took it for granted that she and Darrell would formalise their lives together sooner rather than later. In the meantime they had opened an arty shop in the village and moved in together in the small flat above it. Alison had kept on the cottage, as much because it had been left to her by her parents and it was stuffed with memories. But her commitment to Darrell had been total. So total that, encouraged by him, she had retired from a string of community involvements.

"Can't you see this place is gobbling you up!" he'd said more than once, and Alison had begun to notice how claustrophobic it could seem. And he'd been marvellous at finding new things to do as they rushed off round the countryside visiting art exhibitions and artists and 'finding out what life's all about'.

Then he had started going up to London to see this or that person, initially for the day, then overnight and gradually staying away longer. There was always a good reason to do with building up their reputation, networking, checking out this or that new name. Then she had found a photograph of him and Shelagh in his wallet, raising glasses to each other in a bar. There was one of those clocks giving the date hanging on the wall. It was a very recent photograph indeed.

When she had challenged him he had not attempted to make excuses. He and Shelagh had coincided at some art exhibition, had a drink together, she had asked him for advice on some show she was promoting, and it had gone on from there. And finally it came out. They were going to try and make a go of it again together. "But we can stay friends, can't we?" Darrell said. Was he really that thick?

At the time of Amanda's death and funeral, Alison had been floundering at the bottom of a black hole. It was the week after Darrell had left. Alison had moved back into the cottage and lost herself in a frenzy of redecoration and gardening.

Now, as she let him in, Sim said "It may well not be your sort of thing. It's just that a mate of mine is organising a willow sculpture workshop on Saturday."

"Willow sculpture?" she repeated blankly.

"Yes, making shapes from willow whips, that sort of thing. The general idea is that we should learn enough to run our own workshop at next summer's festival. The guy who's running it is offering a special rate of seven people for the price of six."

"Like loo rolls."

"Mm, something like that. We did have seven. People, not loo rolls; but someone's had to drop out and it's short notice to fill the gap."

"OK." Well, it was something different and she had to rejoin the world some time. "Do you want a coffee?"

Sim shook his head. "Things to do, I'm afraid." Sim always had things to do, usually rescuing people with ailing computers. Perhaps it was his way of coping with loss.

It was arranged that they should travel in two cars. Georgina was going with three from the PTA, Sim said he would take Jill and Alison.

As it turned out, Jill was a good person to make up the third in the carload as she did not stop talking. Mostly it was about the forthcoming village festival on whose committee she was a prominent member. It was agreed that there was real talent in the village, mostly of the musical kind. At least two people were professionals – an oboist and a violinist - retired from major orchestras in other parts of the country. They had an excellent choir, an up-and-coming composer. Then there was the art group, one of whom had been hung in the R.A. And there was Jill herself who was no mean cook and was featured on a local television programme entertaining a group of celebrities in her own home.

"What about you, Sim?" Alison managed when Jill at last paused for breath.

But before he could answer, Jill was already informing her that the festival would collapse if it were not for Sim's skills in ensuring the sound systems were working in the church, the setting for most of our concerts; and the lighting system in the village hall, venue for the art exhibition not to mention sundry craft displays.   By the time she had finished, they had reached the venue for the workshop.   Several other groups had already arrived and settled in various parts of a large shed.   Their mentor led them to an empty area, showed them the various bundles of willow whips, explained briefly what to do, demonstrated some knots and then left them to it.

The whips seemed to have a life of their own as Alison tried to exercise control over them.   Around her murmurs of protests faded into silence of concentration. Glancing round after a while she saw recognisable shapes emerging before hunched figures.

She looked up to find Sim watching her. "You're good at this," he said, a statement, not a question.   "But of course you ran that arty place for a while, didn't you?"

Dangerous ground.   Alison concentrated on weaving the end of a whip into the circle which formed the right ear of the bear she was creating.

"What happened to that fellow – can't remember his name.   The one that used to work for you?" *Not an assessment that would have pleased Darrell.*

"Oh he and his wife moved away from the area."

"Oh, I thought that …   Never mind, I was obviously wrong." *You and I, both.*   "So what's happening to the shop?   Sometimes when we were passing, I'd peer in and Amanda would remind me that I'd once been rather keen on water colours and stuff…"

"Really?"

"Not that I was any good.   I just liked the idea of capturing moments, so you could make 'em last forever, bring 'em out and dust your memories. Amanda didn't paint, but was into arts and crafts in

93

whatever spare time she had; that is, before …. before she fell ill. She was ace at making things: rag dolls, puppets. And tapestry. It was the thing she minded most as she lost the use of her hands. I remember us on country outings: me with my art block, Amanda with a bagful of bits and pieces. I guess that's what I wanted to capture, some of those good moments. Silly really."

It was the longest speech she had ever heard him make. "Not silly at all. It's how a lot of artists feel." Well, Darrell hadn't. He was into post-post-Modernism and you needed to be a mental Houdini to try and grasp what he was getting at. But fair enough. She returned her attention to her work in progress, deftly twisting a frond of willow to anchor her bear's right ear.

"I used to have bear," Sim said unexpectedly. Alison found herself pressing her lips together to suppress a grin. He looked at her severely. "Now you're laughing at me. It's because I look large and tough."

"I have a bear too. He only has one eye and one ear is almost off."

"A bear after my own heart." Sim touched her shoulder briefly and then moved off. She noted he spent a lot of time talking to each member of the group, but an especially long time with Georgina who always managed to seem the odd one out. He was that sort of nice person who would want everyone to feel included.

They had a break for lunch, and admired each other's handiwork. The most popular choice of subject proved to be a bird, and handsome many of them were too, if sometimes a bit wobbly-legged. Jill had gone for a kind of cage rising out of a basket from which you could train a trailing plant.

It was Jill who demanded "And how about you, Sim?"

"I'm just the chauffeur." But they would not let him get away with that and finally, sheepishly, he produced from behind a partition something tall and gangling.

"It's another bird," Jill pronounced.

"An ostrich someone suggested.

"An emu," said someone else.

But no bird had a head and neck like these.

"It's a giraffe," Alison said, and Sim's grin confirmed she was right.

Everyone agreed it had been a great day out. Alison could not remember a time when she had gone so many hours without fuming about Darrell.

----oOo----

The following year it was decided that the Festival willow workshop would be held in the gardens of Manorfields Care Home. On the following day there would be an organised walk down to the local Millennium wood, with optional picnic, and the results of the willow workshop would be scattered about the wood with a prize for the one voted the best. Alison planned to place her bear in a tree.

Sim had made himself responsible for ordering the bundles of willow needed for the workshop, and when she offered to collect them from their source in the next county he said it was okay, Georgie had already said she would do it. Georgie? Ah, Georgina.

During the run up to the festival, life suddenly became busy. Whether Sim had put the idea into her head, or whether it had been there all the time, Alison decided to reopen the shop but broaden the focus to arts and crafts generally. Jill's Mum who headed the county arts and crafts association was almost overwhelming in her enthusiasm and advice, not to mention her contacts who filled Alison's answering machine and email box with recommendations of what she should stock and where she should obtain it. Alison planned to reopen the shop after the Festival.

The willow workshop was planned for the first week-end of the festival. Sim set it up on a fortuitously fine day and by lunchtime the gardens of Manorfields were buzzing. It was quite complicated as the willow whips had to be kept damp or they were too stiff. David had rigged up a king of plastic bath in which to soak them. The kids from the primary school were the most enthusiastic, producing a preponderance of fish and caterpillars. Some of the fish acquired a mast and scrap of material and turned into yachts. Birds were popular of amazing variety and proportions. Sim wandered from creator to creator looking increasingly satisfied.

"How about a willow craft section in the shop," he said to Alison as she helped a 12-year-old with a particularly recalcitrant peacock's tail.

Why not? She could establish a supply with the growers. She could even start a class in basic willow sculpting. She began filing away in the back of her mind various ideas for further thought. For the moment the appeals of "Please Miss, what do I do now?" or "Allie, give us a hand with this," had her scuttling all afternoon. There was hardly time to notice anything else, except that Georgie was doing a lot of scuttling too: a new Georgie, brisk, confident as she kept an ever-growing record of everyone's creations and provided labels by which to identify them when they were set up in the Millennium Wood later. Once she saw Georgie and Sim absorbed in discussion and felt a twinge of envy. Georgie was gesticulating and animated in a way Alison had never seen before. It reminded her of her early days with Darrell. Darrell. She hadn't thought of him for a very long time.

Next day the walk to the Millennium Wood gathered momentum as it proceeded through the village. Many people came as families, some with dogs, most with picnics. Sim and Georgie had made a great job of displaying the willow sculptures, and the wood rang with excited cries as youngsters found their creations and showed them off. Alison found her bear jauntily perched in the fork of an ash tree. She settled beneath it with her picnic, feeling a surge of contentment at the success of the event and a sense of being part of something worth while.

"It's great news about Georgie, isn't it?" Sim's voice said from above her.

"What about Georgie?"

"She's been offered a place on some posh estate in the Midlands. Overseeing a new garden centre."

"Good Lord."

"No, not surprising. She has really good ideas when you can excavate your way through the layers of diffidence."

Alison thought for a while. "And you're good at that, aren't you? Getting under people's skin." She stopped, laughed as she realised what she had said, added, "In the nicest possible way, of course."

Sim grinned back. "Yeah, you could put it that way. Mandy used to call me an interfering so-and-so."

"Mandy? Oh, Amanda. I've never heard you call her that before."

He looked wry. "It was strictly forbidden when we were kids. She could shorten my name to Sim, but then Mandy was an angel and could always get away with anything as far as Ma and Pa were concerned."

Alison found she was staring at him, open-mouthed, got herself under control. Ma and Pa? Sim and Mandy were brother and sister?

But Sim was still talking. "I came to agree with them when our parents were wiped out in an accident. Mandy just took over. She was only a couple of hours older than me, but she always did get the hang of things quicker than I did. Well, girls do grow up more quickly, don't they?"

Alison murmured something noncommittal, then managed "How old were you?"

"Twelve, rising thirteen. I don't think I'd have survived those years on the farm without her."

"On the farm?"

"We were sent to an aunt and uncle in the north. The farm was OK, spectacular hill setting. But aunt and uncle were dire. They'd had a hard life and didn't see why it should be any different for us."

"So what happened?"

"After school, Mandy did a business studies course, I went in for computer technology, so we started a desktop publishing service: fliers, cards, posters, booklets." He paused. "Then she started dropping things, losing her balance." He paused again. "It was pay-back time."

Alison found there was a lump in her throat. "What a wonderful relationship."

"Mm. Mandy had a man in a her life for a bit, but he soon disappeared when she fell ill." He stopped. "Sorry, I have been rabbiting on. And it looks as though people are beginning to clear up." He pushed fingers through his brown thatch of hair. "We'd better give a hand." He began to stride away, paused, turned.

98

"I've got some ideas for the shop opening next week. Fancy a drink and a bite when we've finished?"

"Yeah," Alison said. "I rather think I would."

----oOo----

Back in the here and now, Sim said "You're daydreaming."

"Mm. Happy daydream. It could've so easily gone another way."

"That's what life is: a succession of things that could've gone another way."

It didn't seem the right moment to start debating the pros and cons of fate versus freewill.

"I think they've switched the telly off," Sim said.

"Let's stay where we are," Alison said.

"Mm. Let's."

BEST MATES

"Married?" I repeated, dismayed. Though, heaven knows, the news shouldn't have been unexpected.

"Mm, that's what usually happens at weddings." Even absorbed in list-making Laura managed to look beatific; also, fortunately, too absorbed to register my tone.

Why couldn't I be happy for her?

"It's probably sour grapes, Babs," Kate said when I confessed. "I can't think of anyone who deserves a break more than your Laura." Kate is my favourite resident at Manorfields Care Home where I go regularly to visit some of the oldies. Of course we're not supposed to have favourites but it's difficult not to. Some of them have become pathological moaners while Kate is so grateful for even the smallest thing done for her. She happened to catch me at a vulnerable moment and she's the sort of person that winkles things out of you.

But then even Kate couldn't understand, even though I'd told her Laura wasn't just my best mate but my co-habitant since Chas dumped me last year - as well as my prop and stay. It would be like losing that extra limb you need for all the most desperate times. As for envy, with my history that went with the territory. When you've lived and breathed someone else's presence for three years and they walk out, you can never look at relationships in quite the same light again.

It was Laura's suggestion after Chas left that I move in with her for a while. Her flat had a huge spare room, ideal for setting up all my web design paraphernalia. "You'll be a breath of fresh air to come home to after a day of manicuring wrinklies," she said. She had recently become roving manicurist for an organisation for the elderly. In fact, she was quite a regular visitor at Manorfields. "We can each do our own thing."

In fact, we soon settled into a cosy cocoon of a routine: taking turns with the cooking, or getting a take-away Chinese or Balti, or eating out.

"Who needs men?" she slurred jokily, calling for a taxi after half a bottle or two and an evening of laughs

And no, I didn't simply replace Chas with Laura (even allowing for the obvious differences), remaining well aware, as I had always been, of her idiosyncracies. She is, for example, a lousy cook, hence all those take-aways. And in her own way, she's quite obsessive. Take yoga: not just a regular weekly class that she wouldn't miss whatever the reason, but daily pre-breakfast practise to the accompaniment of much resonating *O-m-m-m-m*. Still, when you live with someone you must make allowances.

Then three months ago she came back from the class and announced "I've met this guy, Bill. Invited him for supper on Saturday. You don't mind, do you? He's doing the cooking."

"You met a man at the yoga class?"

"Don't be so parochial, Babs. He's been coming for the last half term. Actually, his shoulder stands are a bit wobbly." Laura giggled, and that really worried me. She's just not the giggling type. She added "But he's a great cook."

I bit my tongue to stop myself asking how she knew. In fact it soon became clear that Laura knew a great deal more about this Bill than you could be expected to glean from a weekly two hours of self-improvement. He was a librarian, widower, son in Canada, daughter and grandchildren in Aberdeen.

He sounded old, but even then it was a shock to open the door that Saturday evening to a wiry individual of medium height without a lot of hair. Laura was right about his cooking though. He'd brought his own ingredients and, in the space of half an hour or so, while I sipped my vodka and lime, and Laura her elderflower cordial, he produced mouth-melting cream of roasted aubergines served with warm pitta bread.

It was an unexpectedly OK evening. Bill wanted to know about my web designing and knew enough about it to ask interesting questions. We wrangled amicably about the comparative merits of their yoga and my gym work-outs. I found myself thinking he'd be a great candidate for a brother, but as to my best mate's lover?

They became inseparable: country walks, pub lunches, craft shows, concerts. Often I was included. It was all very comfortable and companionable, and not a bit like it had been with Chas and me. Maybe that's why it came as a bit of a shock: the announcement that May 15 was to be The Day, after which Laura would move in to Bill's three-up and two-down on the edge of town.

"It makes much more sense for you to have your own set-up," Kate said sensibly. "Can't you find a nice young man at your gym? I sometimes think that coming here is making you old before your time."

Her daughter, who's into catering, took on the buffet for about twenty in a private room at a local hotel; and the flower arrangements.

There were the wedding outfits to buy and I was in on all of it from the tip of her crushed strawberry

Manos to the matching cloche hat; and, in between, the cornflower blue silk with mandarin neckline and swirling skirt. Of course I was. I'm her best mate aren't I? I allowed her to parade in it once back at the flat before putting it all away. She looked terrific. Her glance met mine in the long mirror.

"I worry about you," she said. "Glued to that thing all day." She meant the computer. Chas had said much the same. More than once.

"I thought of applying for a tutoring job" I said off the top of my head. "At that new college in the ex-stately home." Perhaps Kate was right and I ought to get out and about more.

The wedding was at midday. We'd spent days packing up Laura's things, ferrying them across to Bill's, and she was so happy it couldn't help but rub off. That morning I got ready quickly myself - pale blue two-piece, a waft of antique rose chiffon at the neck - then went to help Laura. She was already dressed, looked perfect.

Then she turned, and I saw the flicker of uncertainty, the uncharacteristic, unspoken plea for reassurance, though what she said was "You will go for that tutoring job, won't you?"

I put my arms round her, gently so as not to disturb the soft drapes of silk, the immaculate fly-away hair cut. "Promise. I'll be fine. It'll all be fine," I said, and felt an engulfing tide of affection for her: Laura, my best mate, my about-to-be ex-co-habitant, my long-ago widowed Mum.

THE CLASS OF '65

As the last strains of a birthday request faded, the local radio presenter said "And now a special message for anyone who was in Briarwood School's Class of '65."

Elli Paterson, busy turning stale bread into crumbs for the birds, paused to stare in astonishment at the portable radio on the windowsill. The voice continued "If that includes you, I gather you won't have forgotten that special year in your lives, at least not according to Pru Travers who's written in to *Contact Line*."

Did you ever forget the summer your best mate stole the first love of your life? And was still married to him by the sound of it. Elli felt herself tense in remembered anguish. After all those years. Absurd.

"Pru doesn't say what you all got up to," the presenter went on, "but she's all for a 50th anniversary and Summer celebration. And she guesses that, as she is still around, it's likely that quite a few more are too. So if you were one of that Class of '65 make a note of July 4th for a wander down memory lane and contact Pru for details c/o us at *Contact Line,* Mid-West Radio. And now here's a request from …."

Elli reached across to switch the radio off and the kettle on.

"Forget it Elli; they're both rubbish," Fiona had said fifty years ago, appalled at the sight of her stricken and inconsolable friend.

Of course it was nothing new: best mates nicking boy friends. But it didn't stop the pain, not least when you were a still diffident rather immature eighteen coming up for air after A-levels. It had always surprised her the way Pru had befriended her. Taken charge would probably better describe their first encounter on the junior playground when Elli was being mildly harassed by a small group who didn't like her accent or her clothes, she couldn't precisely remember which. "Push off," ordered a small whirlwind with flying dark curtains of hair, who had then turned to Elli. "I'm Prudence," it announced. "And I'll be your friend."

Had any girl ever been more misnamed! They'd become inseparable, Elli the follower, Pru the leader in escapades that had them in trouble more than once. In time it had become clear even to Elli that her own low-key behaviour patterns acted as the ideal foil for Pru's need to be in the spotlight. And it hadn't mattered a bit. Until Jules came on the scene.

Elli poured herself a glass of wine. She'd come across the old album of school photos recently when she moved into the new flat in the residential complex that was part of the Manorfields Care Home and her first (and presumably last) proper home since she returned to England a few years ago. She remembered wryly that at one time she had come very close to consigning the album to a rubbish tip. Now she fished it out from the back of the wardrobe, carried it to the living room, took a sip of tea, opened the album at its last page.

The Class of '65. There she was with a big grin on her face. Hadn't known what was coming to her then, had she? On one side of her was Fiona, the only one she'd kept in touch with. On the other side Pru whose dark curtains of hair had by then long been replaced by a gamine cut that seemed to make her big blue eyes bigger and bluer than ever. In the row behind them was … what was the name of that rather lumpy boy with the slight stutter? Martin? No, Mark. Mark

105

Rogers. She'd rather liked him, but Pru said he was a waste of time. Beside Mark was Jules, gazing back at the camera with a look that she could now recognise as arrogant.

Elli took another sip of wine. It was a long time since she had thought, *really* thought, of Jules: outrageously goodlooking, good at everything and, quite mind-blowingly, interested in *her*. Looking back it was quite obvious: he had the same instinct to protect, lead, dominate that first drew Pru to her all those years earlier. He'd taken her out a few times: a movie, some country rides in his old banger to a country pub or two, a couple of raves she convinced herself she enjoyed. For a few weeks she felt airborne. Then she caught them in the sort of clinch she didn't want to know about: Jules and her best mate Pru. Behind the bicycle sheds if you please! What a cliché!

The phone rang making her jump. "I don't suppose you've been listening to the local radio?" said Fiona's voice.

"Actually I have," Elli said. "And no, I'm not going."

"Pity, I think you'd find it interesting, especially since you've done far more exciting things than most of the rest of us." A pause. "Anyway come for a Balti soon. The twins'll love it. Me too. Next Saturday?"

Firmly Elli went back to the carrots and celery she was cutting up for a casserole. In her mind she surveyed the Class of '65 as defined by Fiona over the years: two now living in Australia, one in Canada, a miscellany of retired nurses, teachers, shop assistants, accountants, a junior doctor; and Mums, of course, including Fiona herself with the gorgeous twins. Well, they were her daughter's twins actually, but spent more time with Fiona than with their single-parent mother.

Then, of course, there were Pru Travers, *née* Matthews, and her husband Jules, their upwardly mobile local celebrities on regional TV. And Mark. She frowned in concentration. Wasn't he something to do with stars, the astronomic kind?

And what about you? Fiona was right – in the end things had turned out OK. More than OK. In due course she had pulled herself together and enrolled on a teacher training course. There had been a few years in a market town junior school and then an irresistible urge to see the world. She'd applied for Voluntary Service Overseas and become a VSO teacher in Nepal.

Her face softened remembering those beautiful children with the big expressive eyes and the mischievous smiles that stretched from ear to ear. At first they followed her everywhere "Hello Lady. Where you from? What is your name? Lady? Where you from?" And when at last in exasperation she had pulled a long solemn face and said "The m-o-o-o-n, I'm from the moon," they had curled up in paroxysms of mirth.

Once they came to know and accept her as part of their daily life, she had marvelled at the intensity of their desire to learn, at the spotless neatness of their school uniforms in which they took such pride, however humble their homes. From the window of her own basic accommodation, she had looked out at views of Annapurna that tourists paid thousands to come and see. And in the temples, beneath Buddha's serene gaze or among the hectic pantheon of Hindu gods, she had found peace.

When her three years were up, she had stayed another two, then another two, until amazingly forty years had passed. Of course she returned regularly home briefly to see her parents while they were still alive, and a few friends. "Goodness you've changed,"

Fiona said admiringly, regularly meeting her at the airport, initially with a very small daughter in tow. Small daughter had grown into big daughter, married, had twins who were the apples of Fiona's eye and who adored Elli. And, yes, she knew she had changed, that all that unconditional affection and respect and sense of purpose had given her a confidence, a sense of ease with the world.

It had been weird when she finally returned to the UK in advanced middle age. For quite a while, sundry nieces and cousins had shuffled her around, a bit like 'pass the parcel'. She had proved quite a useful house-sitter, child-sitter, companion for very elderly mothers or aunts on holidays. But she had also become aware that she could not remain rootless forever, and that the arthritis whose first twinges had marked her last days in Nepal was gathering momentum in England's danker climate. Then Fiona had told her about Manorfields: its retirement flats and small bungalows from which you could eventually moved into permanent residential care.

----oOo----

"It's going to be at The King's Arms," Fiona told her over the Balti the following Saturday. "The Class Reunion that is. Drinks first, buffet supper. I gather there'll be at least one coming from Oz. And remember Becky? She's launching some initiative for sponsoring school kids in Bangladesh. She'd appreciate your input. And you did you say you were in the market for something purposeful."

"I'm *not going* Fiona. I put all that school stuff behind me long ago."

"Are you sure about that?" Fiona said.

Later Elli had gone up to read a story to the twins, now six, who fixed their gaze upon her face, following every expression, every muscle movement. They reminded her of a pair of her favourite Nepalese kids, though she never admitted to favourites. She still kept in touch with some of them, heard about their careers, their marriages, their children. What had Fiona said about Becky? Sponsoring school children in the developing world was a really good idea, both for sponsors and sponsees. She could certainly give her some ideas.

"Perhaps I'll give Becky a ring about the Bangladeshi business," she said when she rejoined Fiona. She caught Fiona's expression, sighed. "OK you win. Where do I get a ticket?"

"I've got two," Fiona said.

----oOo----

Confronting Pru all those years back had been one of the most difficult things she had ever done. It took two sleepless nights and a third day of manipulating an opportunity to get her alone. Eventually she cornered her in the washroom where Pru's full concentration was on applying a pale lavender eye shadow.

Their glances met in the mirror. "Hi partner," Pru began breezily. "Want to try this?"

Elli fought to control the shake in her voice, prayed with her whole being she wouldn't burst into tears as she said "I saw you with Jules."

"Oh." Pru dropped her gaze, turned slowly. "I didn't want that." In the small pause that followed Elli could almost see her rearranging her face before she went on slowly, regret shading into gentle compassion "But you know Elli, Jules really isn't right for you. I mean really. I guess he thought you were a bit of a

109

challenge – out of his usual class. And you are. On a different planet. You'll be glad in the end." With hurt and disbelief Elli watched the process of Pru actually persuading herself that she was doing her friend a favour. Then Pru gave a little appealing smile. "Trust me."

"You're sick," Elli had managed to say before she stumbled into one of the cubicles and slammed the door.

----oOo----

As the New Year approached she began bitterly to regret her decision. She told herself that those years abroad had left her with little in common with her one-time peers. But she knew that was nonsense. They were as likely to be as interested in her as she was fascinated to know, for example, how come flighty little Brenda had turned into an accountant, or that oaf Kevin into a doctor specialising in kids. And what about Mark and his stars? Her mind skidded purposefully across Pru and Jules.

"I'll meet you there," she told Fiona and arrived intentionally late. From the level of noise as she approached the bar, the party was obviously well under way. She found a vantage point from which to observe without being seen, found herself grinning at how some of them had grown into almost adult caricatures of their earlier selves; while others might have been total strangers. No sign of Pru and Jules.

"Assessing the battlefield? I see we are of like mind," a voice said behind her.

She looked round to find a tall loose-limbed man, seventyish, in designer denims watching her with an amused expression. The face was almost familiar.

"It's Elli Paterson isn't it? Though I doubt I'd have guessed if Fiona hadn't mentioned you were

110

coming." He nodded towards the animated gathering. "Living in the area still, I bump into quite a few so it probably doesn't come as quite such a shock.."

And then Elli knew who it was. "Mark – you're Mark Rogers. My goodness …"

"… how you've changed," he finished for her. "You, too. You used to be such a timid little thing."

"And you used to be considerably lumpier."

They laughed. He had a nice laugh that used up his whole face. He said "I decided to take myself in hand. Get a life, as they say; and lost the stutter in the process."

"I guess that's what I did too. Not about the stutter but about getting a life. Well, well. You must tell me about your life with the stars some time."

Mark nodded. "I gather you're at that Manorfields place. I'm beginning to creak a bit myself and was wondering about putting my name down for one of their self-catering units." After a moment he added, "He always was rubbish," and following his glance Elli saw Jules, glass in hand, and Pru beside him: both laughing, looking affluent, well-groomed.

"He's put on weight," Elli said.

"You mean fat," Mark said. "And she's become very loud. As in over-the-top."

Elli giggled, a full-blooded giggle like Nepalese kids did. She said, "Come and have tea with me at Manorfields and you can check the place over."

"Mm. I'll do that."

They saw Fiona waving at them urgently.

"Shall we go in?" Mark said, and held out an arm.

Elli took it. "Let's," she said.

LONG SHADOWS

"A call for you Miss Bingham. From New Orleans."

I don't know anyone in New Orleans Fiona Bingham thought. Still, risen stars in the publishing firmament would naturally take transatlantic calls in their stride. Especially on the day of a major book launch. So she said "Right, put them through," and settled deeper into the leather armchair in her 5-star suite.

From the mirror on the wall by the writing desk, her reflection returned an appraising gaze. Good legs, slim figure even now. And yes, she had been right to change out of the flame trouser suit. Too brash, too confident, especially for the purveyor of moral tales and, even though everyone said she was simply marvellous for her age, not really the most suitable colour for only just the right side of eighty. Besides, the two-piece in self-deprecating eau-de-Nil should look well against the dark midnight blue and gold of the décor in this stately home hotel just outside Oxford.

She put on her pleasant voice. "Good afternoon, Fiona Bingham speaking."

A crackle. A pause. "Hi Fi!" A giggle. "Hey, doesn't that sound kinda cute. Hi Fi!"

Fiona Bingham allowed a frown to creep into her voice. "I beg your pardon?"

The giggle subsided. "Sorry. I've gotten over-excited actually *hear*ing you after all these years. But I guess now you're so well known you won't even remember little me: Upper Fifth, Horbiton High School? Stinko?"

The frown deepened. "Is this some kind of joke?"

"No, truly – it was your idea. Weren't you always the smart one with words? MUM, acronym for Marion Ursula Merrivale. Like the deodorant? QED Stinko. Took a year to live that one down." The next chuckle sound marginally less amused. " Before that I was plain Merry."

Good God. A cameo floated into Fiona's mind: a pale face in a cloud of auburn hair, freckles, green eyes. Anxious green eyes. And nice. Excruciatingly nice. How she'd been infuriated by that niceness – or more precisely by the artistic talent that went with it. A greater talent by far than her own; and Merry hadn't even been aware of it. Greater in an untamed way that Fiona's calculating temperament could never aspire to.

But she'd fixed all that.

Now she protested "Merry, my dear. Good heavens, was I really such a horror? In which case it's all the more darling of you to call all the way from New Orleans. What are you doing there anyway? And how did you know where I'd be?"

"Saints alive, I'm *from*, not *in*, New Orleans. I'm *here*. I've come to Oxford to be part of your great day. I - we've been back in the UK for quite a while now. My Barnie isn't too well and, well, it seemed time to make life easier for us both. So we've come home to our roots and found a great little place - Manorfields Care Home - to retire in Donnington. Do you know it?" Oh yes, Fiona knew it all right: just a few miles from her cottage."Anyway no way would I miss your launch. And seeing you. It's *so* exciting after all these years." The breathy voice became more twangy by the syllable.

"But how on earth did you ….?"

"… track you down? Yeah, I'm real proud of that, Fi. Barnie, he always says once I get fixated on something, nothing …but nothing … will stop me. I'm

113

so crazy about those kids' books of yours, that won all the prizes – and especially those fan*tas*tic pictures. My grandkids adored them. You wouldn't believe how everyone back in the States has gotten hooked on them. Not just kids. *Everyone!* The Thuggie parties and Thuggie clothes and Thuggie clubs? I just love those Thuggies and how they always come out good with their big hearts, however *bad* they behave. And, of course, that's where you hit the jackpot, eh?. I guess every kid is a Thuggie at heart."

Fiona's reflection in the mirror became reminiscing. She didn't often have occasion to revisit that long ago time of her late teens before the Thuggies were born. She had just come through a miserable end of year period: miserable because yet again she'd been sidelined – by Merry of course - in the school's annual Art Expo. Disconsolate and resentful, she had wandered into that higgledy-piggledy shop tucked away in an alley behind Horbiton market square. Her steps were surely guided for it was not the sort of place that would normally have drawn her; but there among the dusty detritus of several generations, she had stumbled upon Samuel Pooch.

Poor Samuel Pooch, of absurd name and much talent, who had died of consumption at the age of 22 in 1851 and spent probably his last pennies self-publishing a handful of copies of a chap-book of illustrated tales. Tedious tales of impeccable morality but superbly illustrated with whimsical children far ahead of their time, just waiting to be rediscovered a century later.

OK, so poor sickly Samuel Pooch had created them, but it was she, Fiona who had had the vision to translate the sickeningly charming little dears into street-wise turn-of-the-21st century urchins. And it was on their sturdy backs that she, Fiona, had shot to the

114

top: translations into a score of languages, games, dolls, ornaments and a soon-to-be TV series.

Merry was dead right. Every kid - and most adults - were Thuggies at heart

Enough. Fiona watched her reflection put a hand up to a spinning head and took a deep breath. "Delighted you're a Thuggie fan too, and I really appreciate your call Merry, but I have to go. Get ready for my grand entrance." She forced a laugh. "You can imagine how it is. Perhaps we could meet for a coffee or a drink some time when you're in Oxford? I have a cottage near here."

"That'd be great, but just let me fill you in on how I tracked you down. Called your publishers, spoke to this guy who explained he couldn't give me your address, but when I told how far back we went, well, he was real glad to invite us to the book launch, and mentioned where you were staying. Hinted maybe this could be a story for a gossip column or two – you know, grand reunion of star author with one-time school buddy. Just fancy!" There was the briefest pause before Merry went on as matter-of-fact as if discussing the weather, "Only of course we never were exactly buddies, were we? I didn't mention of course how you hijacked my beau." The next pause was longer. "So how is Miles? Are you guys still married? That photograph in the paper sure didn't flatter him – or has he really put on so much weight?"

Suddenly Fiona wasn't amused any more. She said coolly "Naturally we're still married." No need to add 'if only just'. "And I certainly don't recall any hijacking, though I do seem to remember you were rather a sensitive, imaginative child – perhaps a little too imaginative in the case of Miles?"

"Oh I was sensitive all right, Fi. And no, the signals Miles was sending out were loud and clear. But he wasn't a match for your scheming, was he? At least, not in those days. Broke my heart when I heard you and he had become an item. While I was doing my Gap in West Africa? Remember?" Merry's voice softened so that Fiona had to strain to hear. "That's where I met my Barnie and we found we had so much in common: human rights, fair play, all that old fashioned sort of stuff. So we married and went on travelling in all those parts of the world where fair play is in short supply. That's why it was a good few years before I caught up with how successful you'd become. Picked up one of your books in a downtown store when we settled in New Orleans and saw who the publishers were. Miles' folks. Then I understood."

In the mirror, Fiona's reflection taughtened, like a coiled spring. She watched it finger the delicate pendant she had unwrapped from its small box only an hour earlier: a teardrop in white gold nestling against her throat. The accompanying note lay on the writing desk. "*Good luck, most Gorgeous Thuggie. I'll be looking for you across a crowded room*" - affirmation that her current conquest, Craig, would be wangling his way out of the bosom of his family to be with her. Never mind that Miles would be there too, with whichever latest bimbo.

The thought of Craig brought a flash of sanity. Why the hell was she letting this woman purporting to be Marion Merrivale from long-forgotten school days harangue her in this way? Briskly she said "I really don't think we have anything more to say to each other, Merry. Whatever burden of imagined slights you may still be carrying from the past ....."

116

"You're right there, Fiona." Merry said, no longer sounding quite so folksy. "The fact is I have absolutely no regrets. We had the greatest life before we settled in New Orleans. And I paint. Water colours. Modest success, but enough."

Fiona saw that her reflection in the mirror was beginning to look visibly harassed. She said carefully, "Good for you. Well, it's been interesting to talk ... "

But Merry hadn't finished. "Did I mention that Barnie was a lawyer? A good one. Then a couple of years ago he switched to publishing too, and his real passion which is children's literature, especially the little gems from the past that never quite made it for one reason or another. Like Sammy Pooch. Isn't that such a quaint name?"

The reflection in the mirror became very still. "As you know he died tragically young, and let's face it, his tales have a certain predictability. But his illustrations. *They* are quite out of this world. Indeed way ahead of their time. Well, of course you already know that. Then he ... Barnie ... did some research, found Sammy Pooch had a younger brother who married and had a son who had a son who had a son and so on through several generations, all called ... guess what? Yeah, Sammy Pooch. Isn't that neat? He was just thrilled when he learned of Barnie's plans to re-publish his Great-Great-Great-Granddaddy's tales - maybe in tandem with some modern counterparts. A sort of Then and Now approach. Perhaps trigger a debate on where plagiarism ends – or begins. What do you reckon? Perhaps you could come and give us a talk at Manorfields some time?"

The silence lengthened. "Fiona, are you still there?"

A HIPPOPOTAMUS IN THE LOWER LAKE

Over lunch, Annaliese leaned across the table and asked something in a confidential tone. Her voice is quiet at the best of times so when she's being confidential she's almost impossible to hear. She repeated what she had said slowly: "....still a hippopotamus in the lower lake?"

The safest and most truthful response to that seemed to be, "I'm not sure"

It was a couple of months since Annaliese had joined us at Manorfields Care Home. I'm what's known as 'on respite', quite frequently as I 'm a depressive and brief stays at the care home usually set me up for reasonable periods of normality. My version of normality is running a desktop publishing business from my cottage in Donnington: greeting cards, calendars, fliers, booklets for local organisations, that sort of thing.

I knew a number of Manorfields residents and staff, partly because I've spent quite a lot of time there and partly because I know their families - in fact quite a few of them have been my customers. There is no doubt that most of us - at Manorfields I mean - are a touch different one way or another; but Annaliese was special. Until recently she had lived independently with a housekeeper in a flat in London until she became forgetful and started to fall when the housekeeper said she could no longer take responsibility for her. Annaliese's family had looked for a care home and settled on Manorfields as being the most suitable, as well as easily accessible via the M40 for regular visits.

Annaliese's past, however, was another territory. Rumours - which are like Chinese whispers at Manorfields - had it that she was born into the aristocracy: foreign aristocracy as it turned out - a German-Slav mix which couldn't have augured well for her during the 1930s version of ethnic cleansing. She had come to England in her late teens early in 1939 by means of the Kindertransport, and had been fostered by English relatives. I don't know why it seemed inappropriate that she had married a Mr. Jones, but less so when he proved to be a diplomat.

I couldn't work her out at all. She was clearly very bright as well as aristocratic. The name Bletchley Park came up in the conversation quite early on, so she presumably had been involved with that most hush-hush of code-breaking places. She also spoke of continued involvement with the United Nations, mainly checking up on the welfare of young refugees from more recent conflicts
. Further confusion arose over her relationships since her father, husband and one of her sons were all called Matthew (or Mathias, Matej, or Matti depending on which language was applicable at the time). Father and husband had both died, and the son was something quite high up in social services. He came regularly to see his mother with two glamorous middle aged ladies who proved to be his wife and his sister. It all added a touch of spice to Manorfields' rather quiet mealtimes.

The combination of bad hearing and confusion led Annaliese to believe that I was connected with a conventional publisher and she spent some time suggesting her interesting life might be worth recording. Given the rumours and her age of 94, this was quite likely, but it was difficult to make her understand that my modest desktop publishing

119

enterprise was unlikely to gain her world-wide renown. Perhaps it was my apparent lack of enthusiasm that caused her to take against me.

"For heaven's sake don't encourage her!" Heather Armitage hissed at me after a particularly tedious session of name-dropping. "She's the most terrible snob." Well, it takes one to know one.

Elli Paterson, who had a more charitable mind, suggested it wasn't snobbish to be proud of your considerable achievements. Robert Sinclair, who had been in Bomber Command in World War Two and had the patience of a saint, gave up on her when she was dismissive to Mary, his wheelbound particular friend at Manorfields. Kat Greene, who had run her own small enterprise until recently, also came in for the down-your-nose look, but gave as good as she got so it was sometimes as well that hearing problems got in the way of comprehension.

The only one who did not voice an opinion on Annaliese was Megan, but then she lived a lot of the time in her own little bubble. And not a very happy bubble at that. Megan was a source of concern to all the Manorfields carers and quite a few of the residents as, when in her bubble, her one aim was to escape from 'this prison they've put me in.' In her happier moods she would erupt into song with a clear voice that did justice to her native Wales. But the most familiar sound of the day was of Megan's walking frame being trundled through the twisting corridors of Manorfields as its owner searched for a new escape route.

"Everyone is here to look after you, Megan," I'd tell her.

"Pardon me?" she would ask as she rarely remembered to put in her hearing aid.

So I - or whoever else - would repeat the reassurance which sometimes she would happily accept, or at other times would make her angry since it confirmed her suspicion we were all part of the plot.

Summer was the most worrying time, for this was when Megan's search for escape took her a dozen times a day into Manorfields' walled garden. This was small, shady and delightful but full of potential hazards in the form of steps which Megan and her walking frame would negotiate in a worryingly wobbly way. When the carers were distracted by other crises, some of the more agile residents kept an eye on her.

It was a surprise, however, when Annaliese became one of them. I first came across her and Megan huddled together at one of the small tables in the garden. Since neither wore a hearing aid and both had quiet voices (except when Megan burst into song) I was curious to know the topic of conversation, and found a nearby shrub to examine and hover by.

As far as I could gather, Megan was describing one of the several small hotels she had managed and "I really need to get back for supper time; the children will wonder where I am." We had all seen "the children", three of them all now in late middle age. Annaliese's side of the conversation referred to her own rather rarefied life style and mysterious references to prison. There was a suggestion that her experience of the latter helped her to understand Megan's stressful delusions that she was in one herself.

It was both curious, interesting and helpful how relaxed the two of them were together. Indeed on the quite frequent occasions that Annaliese was collected by a friend or relative for an outing, Megan was quite a lost soul, requiring a good deal more attention from everyone else.

"Anna has been sent away," she would tell anyone who would listen, and it would take constant reassurance and Annaliese's eventual reappearance to calm her. And it was Annaliese who found a partial solution by getting permission from Siobhan to take Megan with her on some of her outings. There was usually supposed to be a carer with Megan when she went out from Manorfields, but given Annaliese's son's elevated position in Social Services, the odd exception was allowed.

I had to admit that Annaliese's concern for Megan was quite touching and I remembered my mother's exhortation that you should never judge a sausage by its skin.. She - that is, Annaliese - also had a curious habit of wanting to give her food to anyone who had not yet been served at mealtimes. She seemed to make a beeline for the more isolated or confused residents and spend time talking to them. Since she spoke so quietly it obliged them to make an effort to understand her, which sometimes led to a two-way conversation. She certainly appeared to have an affinity with the less privileged. I decided that it must be something to do with having lived or worked in refugee camps.

And then one Sunday Megan disappeared. A carer went to check her room, another the lounge. No Megan. Nor in the garden. There was no way she could have got out of the garden or gone through the front door which had two bolts and required a strong wrist. Unless a visitor had inadvertently left it open.

Unease gradually deepened to worry, anxiety and alarm. Siobhan had taken a well-earned break and had delegated responsibility to a team of senior carers. Every room was checked, even the most remote and rarely used store rooms. After lunch the second shift of carers joined in the search. It was then that one of them clapped a hand to her head and exclaimed, "Oh Lord! Sorry, sorry!! Annaliese told me yesterday she was thinking of taking Megan on an outing."

"On an outing? Where?"

"I don't know. Some stately home belonging to a friend of Annaliese. You know how Megan keeps on about having to get home to look after the children. Annaliese thought it might distract her if she got her son to take them both for a drive."

"How very unexpected," I said, even as my mother's voice in my head exhorted me not to judge sausages and skins.

At eight o'clock Annaliese returned. Her son got out to extract two walking sticks and a walking frame from the boot, then opened first the front passenger door, then the back. With his help, Annaliese emerged slowly from the front; and then, even more slowly, the welcome figure of Megan from the back.

Once upright, she stood wobbling by her walking frame. "It's been a wonderful day," she exclaimed to the relieved welcoming party of carers and residents.

And then added joyously her face flushed with pleasure, "And would you believe, there was a hippopotamus in the lower lake!"

THE MOUNTAIN

There were days when she missed Jake at that level between the conscious and subconscious that permeated all thought. Some counsellors said that was when you had to challenge it, replace it with more immediate, positive thinking. Others said 'go with it'. And that's what Meg chose to do, allowing herself the luxury of the best of all her memories and discoveries that had defined what she and Jake had been and had yet to become. The strangest things could trigger them. That afternoon the lady who did the flower-arranging at Manorfields Care Home gave a demonstration. As soon as she saw the burst of colour, Meg had hurtled back ten, no fifteen years.

She had been standing on the balcony of their room in the Pension Triglav, thigh-deep in window boxes overflowing with petunias and geraniums. Below her was the lake in which the Slovenian scene before her was mirrored to perfection: alpine meadows rising gradually, then more steeply to soaring peaks. A movement caught her eye, and she found herself observing a woman, quite a bit older than herself, with a panier over her arm. She was moving slowly through a meadow pausing from time to time to pick something and add it to her panier. Meg thought how wonderfully peaceful it must be to be a woman with a panier walking through a meadow of flowers.

Meg looked back at the mountains. "I'm a terrible fraud," she told them.

"What's that?" Jake said, coming out of the shower. As she turned to him Meg thought *any seventy-something would give a lot for a figure like that*. He looked more like a fit fifty, but with an expression of suppressed excitement more suitable to a schoolboy.

"I was talking to the mountains," Meg said.

"Plenty of time for that," Jake said, still rubbing himself vigorously as he came to join her on the balcony. "I think I'll nip over to the tourist office of this unpronounceable place and get some local gen." He stood looking at the view. The woman with the panier was still moving slowly the meadow. "Fantastic," Jake said, but he was looking at the mountains. "Wasn't she a clever girl?"

'She' … Rebecca … their computer-wizard daughter who had turned up three months earlier waving a sheaf of print-outs. "I've found just the place. On the Net. A new mountain for you and Dad and that Golden Wedding celebration." Meg found herself gazing upon superb mountain scenes under the banner heading *The Magic of Slovenia*. Rebecca was still enthusing, delighted with herself. "That's the one – Triglav, the highest in the Julian Alps. Near the Austrian border with Slovenia. It means three peaks, so that'll keep you busy."

And Meg had felt her heart begin to sink.

They had met on a walking holiday in Austria. Meg, just out of business college, had been talked into it by a supposedly best mate who had then cried off at the last moment. Jake was the group leader. Meg had never been a walker in any meaningful sense, but in those days she was pretty fit, fancied Jake something crazy, wanted to impress. And had never turned her back on a challenge.

"Hey, slow down," he'd said on that first day. "The real trick is to find the right pace, nice and steady, so that you can keep it up all day." She hadn't listened of course, and surged ahead in sharp side-stitching

125

bursts with breaks just long enough to stop her heart exploding through her ribs. They'd caught up with her in a state of collapsed immobility three-quarters of the way up. But he hadn't said, even implied, *I told you so*, and by the end of the fortnight she had never felt fitter. Or more besotted. Before they all dispersed on their return to Manchester Airport, they'd made arrangements for a week-end in the lakes. And were married within the year.

----oOo----

"I reckon a gentle trot round the lake for our first day," Jake said over a pork ragout and dumplings that evening. "Get the feel of the place and give our leg muscles a work-out at the same time." He slid the local map across the table. "I was talking to young Ivo who knows all the routes up Triglav. He's promised to sort out the easiest one for you. By the way, his grandfather was apparently a well known botanist in these parts. Killed in the Second World War. And his mother was born in a concentration camp." He shook his head. "Reckon we don't know how lucky we are. Here, pass your glass over."

After her third glass of tangy Slovenian Riesling, a gentle lake-side trot sounded like a profound blessing compared with the full day of mountain slog she had dreaded. And an ideal opportunity to prepare the ground.

"You'll have to make allowances," she said. "I doubt I have the stamina of the old days – well, it's not reasonable to expect it really."

"Codswallop," Jake said comfortably. "Never to my dying day will I forget the way you shot up those Austrian mountains. *But that was half a century ago.* "Not to mention a good many others since." *But it got harder and harder.* Only how did you get that message over to someone who, for all their many other loveable qualities, never for a moment doubted they were right?

For several years, child raising – Rebecca first, then Jake junior and Tommy in fairly quick succession – had provided the perfect justification for bucket-and-spade holidays by the sea. Jake joined a climbing club and periodically went off to do his own thing. And Meg discovered gardening. In due course she began to win prizes: local at first, then county. Their garden was featured on a local TV programme and listed in *Gardens you must visit*. She became gardening correspondent for the local paper.

The time came when the kids began clamouring "to go with Daddy on the mountains". *Why can't they settle for something normal,* she would mutter breathlessly to herself as she struggled to keep up with them on some week-end or summer trip to the Lakes or the Cairngorms or, in due course, further afield to the Jura, the Oberland, the Alps. *Why can't they all take up stamp collecting? Why couldn't Jake develop a passion for golf or some nice gentle spectator sport like cricket?* But he didn't, course. Nor did he seem to notice her new problem with heights. It got worse gradually.

"But it's safe as houses," Tommy would protest, jumping up and down on some narrow ribbon track to prove his point.

"Cut that out," Jake would rap out, then add quietly to her, "But he's right. It's absolutely safe. Do you really think I would put you at risk?" He seemed deeply put out at the idea.

What none of them could understand was that the safety of the track was not in question. It was the magnetic pull of that great void of space between her and the distant valley, or the sea crashing on rocks way below, or that spaghetti ribbon of river at the bottom of the gorge. She could feel the pull of it, the mind-swirling sensation of dropping into space.

But she'd never given up on anything in her life and was not going to start now.

----oOo----

On the way to the lake next morning they passed the house of the woman Meg had seen collecting wild flowers. It was small and charming with window boxes of geraniums, and wood neatly stacked under an overhang. She noticed there were racks where the woman had spread some of her plants to dry. The 'garden' was a small pasture with apple trees and free-range chickens, and a strip of vegetable plot in which the woman was hoeing. She looked up and smiled as they passed.

It would have been a perfect day if Meg had not recognised it as a warm-up for more ambitious ventures. Encircled by mountains, the lake shaded from blue-black through purple to turquoise. They picnicked on a gravelly beach and watched a cable car glide up and down the mountainside opposite. A kingfisher passed in a flash of azure, and trout of no mean proportions slid through mirror-clear water.

It seemed the right moment to say "Think I'll have a day off tomorrow."

Jake looked surprised but said, "OK, love. Then we'll do something a bit more challenging. Got to get into training for the Big One." The Big One. Triglav. 2863 metres, 9393 feet.

He left early next morning to reach for some unpronounceable summit. Meg headed for the meadows, knowing that there, at least for a time, all other concerns would find a different perspective.

128

Close to, the profusion of colour, variety, texture was breathtaking beyond words – you could get drunk on such a sight. She sat on a large smooth rock and began counting the species, comparing them with the organised profusion of her own garden beds, and reached out to touch one of her favourites. It was lovely to see them out in this magnificent landscape.

"*Astrantia major,*" a voice said and she turned to the pleasant wild flower-collecting woman approaching with her panier. A pleasant wild flower-collecting woman who knew Latin.

Meg smiled back. "And do you also speak English?"

"Yes, but I do not know all flower names in English."

"We call this astrantia, too, and I have some in my garden. In fact, I have nearly all these in my garden." Meg waved an arm to embrace the whole meadow. "Cornflower, scabious, ox-eye daisy, campion, trefoils." She laughed. "Sorry, I can't remember all the Latin names. But why do they look so much better here?"

"Perhaps because the grass seems always greener in other pastures. Do you have that saying, too?"

"We do." Meg looked at her in admiration. "Your English is amazing."

"I was an au pair in your country when very young. And, as for the flowers, my father was a botanist."

Ah! "So you are Ivo's mother?"

She nodded. "Yes, I am Marija. And you are staying at the Pension with my Ivo. I have seen you on the balcony." She put her panier down and sat on the rock beside Meg.

129

Meg looked up at the mountains. She said, "My husband is quite determined we should climb it. Triglav, I mean."

"They say you cannot be a true Slovene unless you climb Triglav. There are ways that are not too difficulty. But long, of course. You must be strong."

Meg said feelingly, "He is very strong."

The woman looked at Meg shrewdly. "But it is not necessary for all to become true Slovenes. Even if, like me, you are a true Slovene! Sometimes it is more important to do other Slovene things: like make good herbal teas and medicines; or honey. Have you seen our bee museum? We make very, very good honey."

"I'd love to know more about your herbal teas and medicines. And honey."

"Then you will come and see me and I will show you." They sat in companionable silence for a while. Then Marija said, "My Jan was very strong, too. It is the way with mountain people."

"And you – have you been up Triglav?"

"For me it is not possible. I have – how do you call a sick head for heights?"

"Vertigo. I have it, too. So how did you persuade your Jan?"

"It was not a question of persuading. I told him." Marija turned to look at the mountain, just the tip of its top visible in the distance. Then she said "Sometimes the biggest challenge of all is to speak your own truth."

----oOo----

Jake had had a great day on his unpronounceable mountain. "How about you?" he called from the shower. "You weren't bored?"

"I had a wonderful time. Met Ivo's mother Marija. She knows all about wild flowers and herbs and honey. She wants me to visit her."

"Good. You could fix something up when we get back from Triglav."

Sometimes the biggest challenge of all it is to speak your own truth. It came out in a scrambled blurt. "You know, love, I really think my mountain-walking days are over. I mean *your* sort of mountain walking. Reaching for the sky. That sort of stuff." She heard the shower stop and rushed on. "What I really want to do is develop the garden. Specialise, you know. Maybe alpines. Not just high altitude stuff, but the meadow plants. I'd learn about the medicinal and food values. Marija knows an amazing amount about it. Maybe even start a small business."

"Team work," Jake said, coming out of the shower, rubbing himself vigorously with a towel.

"Team work?" Meg repeated blankly.

"Collecting seeds for your specialist nursery. You concentrate on the meadow plants, I'll collect the alpines." He warmed to the idea. "You'll need to teach me about collecting seeds, storing them. That sort of thing." Meg watched as he draped his damp towel over the bottom of the bed and began dressing. With one leg in and one out of his trousers, he went on, "We'll probably need to get some equipment, but your new friend can tell you about that. I could start practising on the way up Triglav." He zipped up his trousers, grinned at her. "What do you think?"

Meg opened her mouth. Then closed it again and smiled. He hadn't stopped surprising her yet. And as long as she went on remembering him, he never would.

131

LOOKING AFTER MOTHER

Beth Jarrold sat in the conservatory of Manorfields Care Home awaiting a visit from her son Tim and daughter-in-law Jane Could it only be six months ago that she had been hiding from them in the cupboard under the stairs, eavesdropping - albeit unwittingly - on their conversation?

She smiled, remembering that the conversation had begun as it always did. As the front door closed behind them Timothy Jarrold had grumbled "This place really is far too big."

In her head Beth added "It's quite, quite absurd."

"It's quite, quite absurd," Timothy said, and she gave a little smile.

From a corner of the wide hallway the grandfather clock ticked loudly through the silence: a curious, waiting silence. Into it Jane said "I'm not happy poking around when your mother's not here."

Timothy frowned his impatience. "Good Lord, we've been trying to ring her for two days. We're simply checking everything's all right. And she's been acting very oddly since she joined that reading group and..." He turned briskly into the living room.

"... met that Henry fellow," Jane murmured following him.

It was a large living room in keeping with the big leather suite, the heavy marble fireplace, the floor to ceiling bookcases, the massive oak dresser.

From the doorway Jane commented, "Amazing how she's managed to make this place her own in spite of your Dad's ... er .. tunnel vision: a bowl of fragrant pot pourri here, a well-placed plant there, a sunlit country scene cheering a dark corner, a bright splashy rug on a gloomy landing...."

Clever Jane, Beth thought to have noticed so much. But now a startled grunt from Timothy and an "O-o-o-o-h!" from Jane indicated they had also noticed the new music centre and its strategically placed speakers. After the silence had gone on for long enough, Jane said, "Well, your mother always was very fond of music."

Dear Jane. It was some time after his father's funeral that Tim had told Beth, "You'll want to move somewhere more convenient."

She'd looked surprised. "But I find this extremely convenient, dear."

Timothy explained patiently, "It's such a *big* place, Mother. There's a splendid residential home near us. Just think, no shopping, no cooking. Just round the corner from the church and the library. We'd be able to see you more often; it would be so much more convenient."

"Convenient for whom dear? Really Tim, I'm not yet in my dotage. Anyway we ... I like this house. I *like* cooking. And I've had nearly forty mostly happy years here. It fits me like a comfortable shoe."

From that brief speech Jane had probably learned more about her mother-in-law than in six years of admittedly infrequent visits since her marriage to Tim. She found she was glad, if surprised, that Beth had been happy with that self-opinionated old curmudgeon who was Timothy's Dad. Timothy's face had taken on a *we'll-see-about-that-later* expression. For a moment he'd looked startlingly like his father.

They had been colleagues, Jane and Tim, in a firm of accountants, gone to a concert or two together, had the occasional dinner. Then one evening she had seen the light on late in his office and found him in tears. It was like seeing Gibraltar crumble. He told her about the elderly neighbour he'd been keeping an eye on unobtrusively since she'd been widowed, and who had died that day. That carefully guarded need to be needed was a vulnerability the rest of the world never saw, and she had loved him for it.

Now, from the bay window she looked out at the garden that had always been Beth's domain. Beyond it the ground dropped away to the valley, merging into rolling farmland that gave a sense of space and continuity. There would be no such views from the retirement flats.

"Someone's keeping the lawn under control," she murmured, knowing exactly who that someone was.

Timothy grunted again and crossed the hall to the study. Here for sure among the papers marking his father's life-long interest in military history he would find echoes of his solid unchanging values.

He stood in the doorway aghast. The solid bookcases, the wooden filing cabinets were still there; but the big oak desk had given place to a light modern one in the centre of which sat a computer. Beth had already forewarned Jane: something about editing the club's newsletter, even trying her hand at a course in creative writing. She'd added, "Better not mention it to Tim just yet; I don't think I'm quite fitting the right image."

You've re-arranged my ideas of it too, Jane thought following Tim back across the hall to the kitchen, modernised some months ago. There were some papers strewn on the breakfast bar. Leafing through them Timothy gave a sharp cry. Beth immediately guessed the reason.

134

"Tim that's prying," Jane protested, but glanced at the letter from a local travel firm. It confirmed a booking on a Greek island in September in the names of Mrs Beth Jarrold and Mr Henry Carruthers.

"Well at least they're not travelling as Mr and Mrs Smith," Jane said, without meaning to.

Timothy exclaimed "Really Jane, I can't think what's got into you."

Contrite she said "I just wish you wouldn't feel so ... so responsible."

Beth, who had pushed open the cupboard door so that she could hear better, hastily closed it as Tim said, "Let's take a quick look upstairs."

"I hope," she stage whispered to Henry, "you put all your stuff away."

"I always put my stuff away," Henry stage whispered back. "Just in case."

Their visitors clearly found nothing untoward as they soon returned to the hall. Jane said tentatively "Shall we go home then?"

Timothy burst out "I can't bear the thought of her going off with that Henry fellow." And added bleakly "I *promised* Father I'd look after her."

So that's what all this was about. Jane put a hand on his arm. "Timothy my love, they gave each other nearly forty years of rock-solid companionship. Your Mum has to live with the loss of that in her own way." She paused, then went on firmly "Anyway I *like* Henry. He has a great sense of humour. Not bad looking either with that silvery beard and hair."

They had met just the once at Beth's for a pre-lunch drink, oh, a couple of months back. Timothy came as near to rudeness as his upbringing allowed and at Beth's urging Jane had whisked Henry off for a tour of the garden.

135

Tim said "You've never said anything about it before."

"You wouldn't have listened." Like father, like son? On an impulse Jane put her arms round his neck and kissed him in a way she hadn't for rather a long time. "But perhaps I should have tried."

Timothy said nothing, but his clasp tightened and they stood for a moment quite still. As the door closed behind them the grandfather clock ticked on into the silent hallway. Then there was a small click. Emerging from the cupboard under the stairs Beth said "Thank heavens you saw the car draw up."

"Not bad looking, eh!" Henry stretched his tall frame.

"Shut up, Henry," Beth said equably. She led the way into the kitchen shaking dust from her hair. "My poor Tim - oh dear, that need to be needed; they were ... are so very alike." She broke off and her expression softened. "They were ... are good men, Henry."

"I know, my dear."

Then she giggled. "Look at us like naughty kids hiding from my own son. And Jane - seems the mouse is turning into quite a wise owl!" Then she added, "And by the glimpse I had of Jane's figure I think Tim will have something else on his mind soon."

Now eight months later, a great deal had changed. Timothy junior was nearly three months old and had become the focus of his father's concerns. The trip to Greece had come and gone and consolidated the deep friendship between Beth and Henry. The former had moved into Manorfields and discovered there were self-contained apartments in the grounds in one of which Henry was to join her in a few weeks time. She was about to tell Tim and Jane.

136

THE NEW BOY

It was Denzil's idea that the Donnington Writers Group should meet once a month in Manorfields Care Home. It would be good for the old folks, he said, and anyway the group's numbers had been depleted by one death and one moving to Australia. The remaining four agreed that the atmosphere was becoming a tad claustrophobic especially as they had become so familiar with each other's views.

"And," Denzil added, "there's a new chap who's moved into one of the flats who's a retired magazine editor and already complaining there's not enough going on to keep his brain from seizing up. Plus a new youngish one who is keen to have a go."

"Youngish?" queried Amy.

"Seventyish,"

"Mm. that is youngish for Manorfields," Maggi agreed. "And we could do with a retired magazine editor."

"And then," Denzil went on, "there's a James Hadleigh-Dean who's emailed me for details of the group."

"He sounds like an estate agent. Or a solicitor," Amy said.

"Wasn't there a film star called James Dean?" Maggi murmured.

"Landscape gardener," Denzil said. "Has published some gardening articles, wants to try his hand at fiction. Got my name from the local library."

They all agreed they needed new blood. Of the right kind, of course. Maggi was a successful writer of short feel-good romances. Amy was deeply learned and won competitions. Denzil wrote clever poetry but

137

not very often. Tom, their newest recruit, was beginning to do well in the children's market. Marcus, the retired magazine editor, had already attended one of the writers' group's meetings and given it his seal of approval. He was, Denzil pointed out, an extremely alert 'old boy', if a bit full of himself and had taken the care home's relative newcomer, seventyish Dorrie, under his wing. It was Marcus' intention to start a workshop at Manorfields to encourage residents to write down some of their early memories.

"In a lot of cases," he confided to Denzil, "their short-term memory is rubbish; but long-term they have remarkable recall and stories to tell which would make the hair of the modern young stand on end."

Yes, well Denzil had already met Jess and learned about the FANYs and had heard of various amazing achievements in the third world by other residents. For most of Manorfields' residents modern technology was a no-no, but he could probably help with some old fashioned tape recorders which weren't too difficult to get to grips with. He could even see possibilities in the idea of turning the memoirs into a publication, or creating a blog on the Internet.

It was decided that James Hadleigh-Dene should attend the first meeting at Manorfields, an opportunity for them all to discuss the future format of the new group. The smaller conservatory had been put at their disposal and the sun shone on a fine array of orchids on the afternoon of their inaugural meeting.

James H-D was the last to arrive. "Accident on the A4321," he said apologetically, thrusting out a hand to each of them in turn.

More like a car salesman than a landscape gardener, judged Amy. A shopkeeper, Maggi assessed.

Tom merely surveyed the rather red-faced stocky middle-aged man without judgement.

"Bit like the first day at school, this is," James went on jovially. "So what's the form? I've brought my test piece as Denzil suggested."

"I suggested he ran one of his gardening pieces passed us," Denzil explained.

The article was about turning a small suburban patch into a wildlife garden. James H.D. did not read very well. The text was lively enough, but lost colour in the monotone of the delivery. When he had finished there was a small silence.

"What a lot of good ideas. Does sawdust really work to keep slugs off favourite plants?" Maggi ventured.

"I thought everyone knew that?" Amy added testily "By the way it's *garrya elliptica:* two 'r's and two 'l's. It's important to get it right."

"Amy means editors won't take on contributors they suspect are unreliable," Denzil said.

"Amy means what she says," Amy said tartly. "Good Lord, you're always going on about accuracy! How about you Tom?"

"Well, I think it has loads of colour and good ideas. I'd like to read it again"

James had brought several copies and handed them round while Denzil went out to organise tea. There were some minutes of silence broken by rustling paper.

"Do you envisage this as part of a series?" Maggi asked. "And for what market? We always think it's so important to have a market in mind."

Amy was frowning. "The trouble is it falls between two stools. There are certainly some nice touches, but it's a trifle self-indulgent if I may say so."

139

James murmured something that sounded like "I'm sure you will."

"How about our newcomers? Marcus? Dorrie?"

Marcus nodded. "Yes, I do have a suggestion. Have you thought of the county mag? I do believe there is a new one. Posh it up a bit with suggestions for tasteful arrangements. Of course it's important that you should study some issues of the magazine so you get the right angle. They'll have copies at the library."

"Yeah, I'll do that."

There was a pause as Denzil returned with a tray of tea and a plate of biscuits.

"What do you think Denzil?"

"Good ideas. I'll certainly import some into my patch. But I'm not good on markets. I leave that sort of stuff to Maggi."

Maggi looked apologetic. "Come up with a steamy romance and I might be able to help. But gardening – no."

"An easy marketable style, don't you think?" Denzil commented after seeing James out.

"Self-opinionated," Amy pronounced. "I can't see him taking advice."

"Well, you'd know about that, wouldn't you?"

"Any market news anyone?" Tom interrupted, ever the peace maker.

"If you don't mind me saying so," Marcus put in, "I thought you should perhaps be more critical of style, over-use of adjectives, that sort of thing. After all we don't want to turn into a mutual admiration society."

There was a brief exchange about the new county magazine and the latest competitions listed on a website. Amy had been shortlisted for one of them and was duly congratulated.

"So," Denzil said, as the meeting broke up. "Shall we invite our double-barrelled friend back?"

"Let's see if he takes up any of our suggestions."

"And how do you think Marcus is shaping up?" Denzil asked when their new member had gone.

Still a bit full of himself was the general consensus.

There was no further news of James H.D. by the time they met the following month, but Denzil had a copy of the local paper. In it, he'd marked up an imminent series for local writers: to be judged by a literary agent with some surprisingly generous prizes. There was, also surprisingly, a reference to potential new material from the elderly residents of Manorfields Care Home which could eventually find a home in a new series in the paper.

Tom was the first to notice. "Have you seen who is researching the series? A new member of staff, a certain Jimmie Dee?"

Maggi looked puzzled. "So...?"

Amy said "Oh Lord!"

Denzil mused "Jimmie Dee, Jimmie Dene, James Dene, James Hadleigh Dene. Yes, Amy. Oh Lord, indeed."

GRANNIES DOT COM

Most of my friends say that old people are boring, but I don't agree. My name is Buzz Radovski - yes, I know that's a bit of a weird name, but my grandpa came from Poland after a big war. That's the Radovski bit. My first name is William, though when I was younger I hated it so called myself Buzz. Grandpa's dead now and I don't remember him, but Granny Em is alive and has some really wicked stories. The only problem is she doesn't hear very well and won't use her hearing aid. She's living in a place where they look after old people now, but until a few months ago she lived in a bungalow in the next street to us.

I go and see her quite often as she has some wicked stories. One of the most wicked, though, I found out by accident. I'm going to tell you about it because in a way it's my story as well as Gran's.

Everyone says I'm dead lucky because Dad is well off. When I asked Mum what Dad does, she said, "He buys and sells stuff," and when I asked "what stuff?" she said, "It depends." She was putting shiny film on her toe nails at the time and I guess didn't feel like discussing it. She was a model once and I've seen pictures of her looking seriously amazing.

Anyway, whatever stuff it was, Dad did all right. We have two cars, a big house in Oxfordshire, a flat in London and a villa in Spain. He and Mum quite often go to Spain, and in the old days I stayed with Granny Em. Dad looked after her money, too, so she had a nice bungalow in the next street to our house and often came to have meals with us.

Dad never said anything nice about Grandpa. Granny Em explained it was because they were 'like chalk and cheese', which I thought sounded funny. Apparently Grandpa was no good at making money, but very good at making music. "Like you," Gran said. Only Grandpa played the violin and I prefer the piano. She said I liked listening to what she called 'good music' even when I was a baby so it must be in my genes.

I loved staying with Granny Em because she'd kept Grandpa's old upright piano ("sit up and beg", she called it), and I could play it as much as I liked. Dad complained when I played at home. He likes all the new groups, and I'm really into stuff like Chopin and Mendelssohn which, I suppose, is what Gran calls 'good music'. Kev thinks they're pretty naff too, and I just can't explain how I feel when I'm playing them: like I'm in a completely different world and what I'm doing is mega important.

"I don't know where he gets it from," Granny Em says sometimes, talking about Dad. "He must be a throwback to *his* grandfather." Apparently he was a bit of a tearaway. Anyway I don't think she likes Dad that much. I once overheard them having an awful row and to make it worse it was about me. Dad was saying she shouldn't encourage me with this music nonsense, and she said really crossly, "You ought to be damn'd grateful to have a son with real talent." I wasn't sure whether I was more pleased by the compliment or more surprised to hear Granny Em swearing.

Soon after that, like, Dad agreed I could have extra music lessons, and as I guessed that it was a lot to do with Gran, I asked her if there was anything I could do for her. To my surprise she said, "Yes, you can teach me how to use this computer!"

It was a quite a good one because this friend who'd given it to her was a bit of a nerd, always wanting the latest of everything. So I taught her the ordinary stuff like sending emails and creating documents.

Three years past. I grew taller than Gran, and Buzz began to seem rather a stupid name, so I changed myself to William. My music was going really well and I even started composing a few bits. I overheard Gran tell someone I was taking after Dad for looks, but thank God in other respects I took after Grandpa.

Initially guided by me Granny Em learned about computers and began to explore cyber space. Then she made experimental forays into chat rooms and forums and newsgroups. Many of these, she told me firmly, struck her 'as a massive waste of energy in which a great many people with not much to say took a mega amount of time saying it'; she also found that some of them got up to some very unusual and not-at-all-nice things. Yes, well I'd discovered that too.

Then she said she wanted to get to know other people; it was quite lonely getting old with friends of the same age dying, like, or moving away to be near their children. So she wanted to find a way of getting in touch with oldies like her in different parts of the world.

"You ought to start a webring, Gran. That's the way to get a *real* online community going," I told her. "I'll help you make your own website." I'd recently developed my own and was in touch with a widening global circle of mates experimenting with digital music.

But when she finally designed something simple and homey, with a picture of herself and her list of interests that included reading, gardening and tapestry I protested "That's seriously naff, Gran."

"I *am* naff dear," Em smiled. "How about calling it <granniesforreal.org>?"

Well, I did a bit of research and found if you put that in a search engine, it led you to some nasty places so I persuaded her to change it and she chose Methuselah's.women.org instead. Of course she had to explain that Methuselah was the oldest man who lived: 969 years - I found that out on Wikipedia.

Within days she was deluged with messages from other grannies gratefully hailing her and each other as the first 'real people' they'd met in cyber space. With a few she exchanged email addresses and with one in particular she found special empathy: a widow called Jezebel in some remote Ozzie outback.

"Is that *really* your name?" was one of Em's first questions.

"Jeez no; but would you have wanted someone called Agatha as a cyberpal? Anyway that was my gorgeous hunk's name for me so it'll always be special." They swapped lengthy life stories, including Em's wish that I should follow my musical star.

"Don't know where we went wrong with my stingy and self-opinionated son," she emailed sadly.

"I'll tell you how to make money," Jezebel emailed back, "Maybe with enough left over to come pay me a visit." Em read on, her eyes widening in disbelief, and clicked it off before I had time to read it properly. I'd seen enough, and was pretty disbelieving, too. But Gran wouldn't, I thought. She wouldn't dare. What Jezebel had suggested was that Gran put pictures of herself on the Web wearing ... well, not wearing very much, and sort of blackmailed Dad. Then she clicked off before I could read the rest. I went back later to check the emails, but she had deleted it so thoroughly I couldn't find it, which meant she had been paying attention to my lessons.

And then it all went out of my mind as the school concert approached. I can't imagine how I allowed myself to be talked into it, but I did. And worse still, my Dad had allowed himself to be persuaded to come to hear me play a Mozart sonata, the centrepiece of the evening. He and Mum were in the front row and I could see him muttering to himself while there was the usual buzz of chatter all around.

I was the first act after the interval and suddenly it was time for me to go on. And, as always, after those first horrendous seconds of walking out on to the stage and sitting at the piano, it was like everything and everyone had gone and there was just me and the piano and the music. When I had finished, there was a silence that seemed to go on forever, and then there was a thunder of applause that was absolutely amazing. When I looked down at the front row, I saw that Dad's mouth had fallen open and then he started clapping and got to his feet, and other people did.

"You're amazing, son," he said with an expression on his face I had never seen before. "And you'll be the star at my promotions one day."

I didn't know what he was talking about until I overheard him telling Mum about his vision of smart hotel conference rooms with chandeliers and thick carpets and mirrors reflecting a gathering of his wealthiest punters, everyone of them with a fat wallet. He could hear the clink of glasses, the buzz of voices and laughter gradually fading as he called for hush and my slender figure settled at a grand piano. "Right," Dad would announce, "the choice is yours my friends - any tune you like, and my William will play it for you." And they'd call 'em out, all the old favourites, rousing and randy, maybe romantic, even something really classical like that Gershwin bloke. People loved it if you could get a good old sing-song going.

Anyway, the evening of the concert, over a glass of wine, my music master said "Delighted to meet you, Mr Radovski," and shook Dad's hand vigorously. "You must know of course that your son is quite exceptional. He has a great future in music. A great future."

I could almost heard Dad's expression saying *no son of mine is turning into that sort of poncy musician* but aloud, he contented himself with "Yeah, he'll keep up his practise, you can be sure of that."

The rows started: that is Dad ranted loudly about how he had had his final say and that he encouraged me to practise as much as I liked but I wasn't going to any academy to learn more poncy music. I sat silent and scowling, wondering how on earth this mega problem could be solved as there was no way I was going to become Dad's performing monkey playing dire music for his friends. Mum fluttered between all of us. I could tell Granny Em was really worried and from somewhere in the back of my head I remembered Jezebel's proposal. Which was unthinkable. Absolutely unthinkable.

And then, I don't know how but she must have done some research on the internet, Gran found out how to take pictures of herself, and asked me if she could borrow my digital camera. Well, since she had given it to me, I could hardly say no. What followed I gathered from checking up on Gran's emails which, on this occasion, she forgot to delete. Apparently she had managed to take a series of photographs of herself and stored them in a file which, try as I might I couldn't find. She must have emailed it to Jezebel (she remembered to delete that one) because next thing her friend was emailing back "Good on you. Tell me when it's up and running, and I'll do my stuff."

And what 'stuff' was that I wondered?

----oOo----

It was a week later and Dad had just returned from one of his innumerable wheeling-and-dealing trips. In the bathroom Mum was taking the hairs of her legs (what weird things some grown-ups do) and humming along with Radio One. As a howl of fury was followed by several really bad swear words she looked up, cautiously opened the door and called "What's up, lover?" But Dad was already slamming out of the house.

He returned an hour later in a silence weighted with suppressed rage. Mum watched him anxiously, instinctively recognising that for once this was no time for playful games.

Over supper he snarled at last "William's to go to this ... this music academy place." He scowled. "Yeah, and the subject's not up for discussion."

Granny Em was quietly satisfied. I was over the moon of course, but also mystified.

When I was sure Mum and Dad would be away for the day, I went to the part of the house Dad had had adapted as his 'office suite' and did a thorough search. Well, they are always telling me I'm untidy but you should have seen the mess Dad's stuff was in. It looked as if he never put anything away, so I didn't have to look far. Slipped into the top of a drawer was an email from which my eye caught Granny Em's name.

It was from Jezebel in Australia. It took me a while to understand what was going on because the email started by saying she was a well wisher who had heard of Dad's reputation (what was *that* supposed to

148

mean?) and assumed his mother's newest venture did not have his approval. Attached to the email was a sheet of paper headed <naturalgrannies.org> with a photograph of Em wearing....

My mouth fell open because, in fact, Granny Em was wearing nothing at all except for a few wisps of material, carefully placed but leaving little to the imagination.

"*Wow!*" I said aloud then read on

Hi! said the text underneath the photograph. *I'm Em and I live in the UK. I need some money for my grandson's studies. Email me if you can help and, in return, I'll tell you more about who I am, where I live and send you some very special pictures.*

"*Wow! Cool,*" I said again, as finally I sort of understood.

BUNTY AND THE PERHAPS-ANGEL

"I'm off," Maddy said to Sue, head cook at Manorfields Care Home, slipping off her apron. On her way she paused at the open conservatory door peered across the garden to a figure bent over the flower beds. "Hi, just off. Don't forget Bunty's bringing the sprog over this evening."

The figure waved an arm in acknowledgement and Maddy headed out of Manorfields towards the centre of Donnington, let herself into one of the cottages overlooking the market place and switched on the kettle. It was part of an almost daily routine: that and the cup of tea she would take out on fine days on to the patio among the tubs of geraniums where she would, as likely as not, indulge in one of her favourite memories. It was a daydream that would take her back twenty-five years.

----oOo----

"Look Mummy, an angel!" Bunty had shrieked that long-ago December, her long fair hair swinging.

All too familiar with the excesses of her daughter's fertile imagination, Maddy Gregson began "Don't be ...." but hadn't got as far as "... silly sweetie" when she stopped. Across the market place with the December sunshine highlighting his white sweater and creating a curious halo effect about his head, the man did look disconcertingly angel-like. Not least because he was playing a very large harp.

As they approached, the sound rippled like dappled sunshine on a woodland stream. Maddy found herself smiling at the sheer pleasure of it. As a piano teacher music was an essential part of her life. By the time they reached him the halo had dissolved and the harpist had paused to attend to an older man who was saying ".... they *will* be pleased Stefan." It was then Maddy saw he was collecting for the local hospice.

"Are you really an angel?" Bunty was hopping from one foot to another.

The older man laughed but Stefan looked at Bunty quite seriously and said "Perhaps one day if I am good enough." Maddy noted the slight foreign accent; then he smiled and she thought *what a very attractive man.*

She turned away. She was through with attractive men, or indeed any other kind. Four years of living with Gerry had seen to that.

But Bunty was tugging at her arm. "*Wait* Mummy, I want to give the Perhaps-Angel some of my pocket money." Maddy paused resignedly while her daughter made a great performance of extracting 50p from the patchwork purse that hung round her neck.

Stefan said "Thank you. You are a golden girl with a good heart."

As they moved out of hearing Maddy said "I don't like it when you show off."

"I *was*n't," Bunty protested. "The Perhaps-Angel was pleased." She glanced sideways at Maddy and added "And I expect Daddy would have been too."

She had discovered quite recently that mention of her father usually cut short any scolding. It worked. Maddy sighed and fell silent as they headed for the car and home. Gerry had actively encouraged Bunty's precociousness; it was one of the many things they had come to disagree on. It was four years now since he had left for New South Wales with a sleek Ozzie redhead over in the UK on a short training course.

151

Though Maddy had fallen out of love with him long before, this sudden and crude rejection had turned her life upside down, blown apart her self-confidence. Only three at the time Bunty remembered him hazily as a Mr Nice-Guy who gave her presents and made her laugh. After days of agonising over what to tell her, Maddy settled for "Daddy's gone to work a long way away in Australia for a while" and hoped that time would do the rest. And, thankfully, for a long while it had.

That evening as Maddy came to the end of her nightly story, Bunty said drowsily "Can we go and see the Perhaps-Angel again?"

"He's just a nice man, not an angel sweetie, not even a 'perhaps' one," Maddy said, but her daughter was already asleep, golden hair splayed out on the pillow looking heart-meltingly like an angel herself.

Maddy went on sitting there quietly, watching her. The fact that she loved her to bits didn't blind her to the precociousness that also showed up in Bunty's writing and drawing skills; and likewise had sometimes tested her teachers' patience to the limit. Getting the balance right between stick and carrot could be really hard when you were responsible for wielding both. Then the difficult questions had begun three months ago.

"Has Daddy died?" Bunty had suddenly asked soon after learning of the death of one of her friends' grannies.

"Of course not," Maddy said firmly. Though how could she be sure? It was well over a year since the last contact.

Soon after came the question she had always dreaded because of the deep-down sense of failure, however unjustified, associated with it. "Mummy, are

152

you and Daddy vorsed?" Bunty asked as she scooped up fluffy mounds of bubblebath one evening. She frowned over the unfamiliar word, and hurried on "Because Jennie Peters said her auntie vorsed her uncle and he went away too."

Maddy reached across for a towel and said quietly. "It's called divorced sweetie, when Mummys and Daddys decided to live apart. And yes, that's what we decided to do." To her relief that seemed to suffice.

Thankfully Bunty didn't seem to remember the rows, increasing in number and vehemence, until they seemed to disagree about everything. How could it have happened? Oh quite easily, Maddy acknowledged when, long ago, she had accepted her own part in it. Infatuation, the dizzy joy that someone as gorgeous and streetwise as Gerry had actually fallen for her had stifled completely the small voice of doubt somewhere deep down.

They had been both so young: still at college, Maddy with her music, Gerry with his sights set on high finance. Far too young to take on board that the attraction of opposites was not always the best basis for a stable long-term partnership. Though she had tried, she really had.

----oOo----

There was no sign of Stefan or his harp in the market place a few days later.

"I expect he's working," Maddy said, quite sorry not to hear that mellow flow of sound.

"Making all those sick people better," said Bunty clearly fostering vivid images of a harp-toting ministering angel. But her attention was soon distracted by the many signs that now presaged not only Christmas but her own birthday. The big Christmas

153

tree from their twin-town in Austria now sparkled in a corner of the market place; stalls were wreathed in tinsel and fairy lights; and wall-to-wall Christmas carols filled the air. In a week's time Bunty would be eight, in two weeks it would be their fifth Christmas without Gerry. Tucked away in Maddy's wardrobe was the Barbie outfit she had made secretly in the evenings after Bunty was in bed; and a small easel to encourage those early daubs which were showing such promise. She had also booked matinée seats at the local Arts Theatre for a revival of *The Sound of Music.*

On the eve of the great day they were indulging in pre-birthday tea and chocolate cake, when a voice from the next table exclaimed "It is the golden girl with a good heart!"

"Mummy, it's the Perhaps-Angel," Bunty was bouncing with excitement.

Maddy smiled. In jeans and bomber-jacket, he looked a good deal more of an earthling than on their previous encounter. He said "It's nice to be a Perhaps-Angel. But otherwise my name is Stefan."

"And I'm Bunty," Bunty said. "And I shall be eight years old tomorrow. And this is Mummy. She plays the piano."

"Happy birthday tomorrow, Bunty." Stefan glanced at Maddy questioningly.

"Maddy Gregson." She gave a rueful smile. "I'm afraid my daughter can be impossibly precocious at times."

"I have a niece in Poland - my sister's daughter. She is very much like Bunty, with long beautiful hair, and likes to pretend she is bold."

"Where is Poland?" Bunty wanted to know. "Is it far? Like Australia?"

Stefan laughed. "Not *so* far, but far enough."

154

"It must be lonely away from your home," Maddy said.

He shrugged. "I came to stay with my aunt and English uncle here at the time of some political problems many years ago. I'd just qualified as an engineer and I was lucky enough to be able to stay. So now *this* is home." He paused. "So you play the piano?"

"I give lessons, and sometimes play for friends."

"You could play together!" Bunty said, clearly pleased with such a clever thought.

Stefan looked at Maddy. "I would like that." Then after a pause that went on too long, he said "But in any case you will find me on the market place most mornings before Christmas."

Maddy shrugged into her coat as she said "We'll probably see you there then. Come on young lady." She turned and gave Stefan a small apologetic smile.

Bunty was lost in a television programme on monkeys that evening when the telephone rang. "Good morning England," drawled a voice Maddy had not heard for a long time.

"Good evening Gerry," she said coolly.

"Yeah. Evening, of course. And here we are basking in early morning sunshine on the terrace, sipping our breakfast orange juice." Maddy glanced at raindrops glinting on the window pane and found she was hugely glad not to be sipping orange juice in far away early morning sunshine. Gerry was saying "So my little Bunty's birthday hasn't yet begun - I was just telling Jaz here about her and she said why not call...?" Jaz? That was a new one. "I guess she must be all of seven by now."

"Eight," Maddy said shortly.

"Is that right? Yeah I guess it's a while since I've been in touch."

Quite suddenly Maddy didn't want to be talking to him any more. She said "I expect Bunty would like to speak to you. But I really don't have anything more to say."

A few moments later she closed the door on the excited "Daddy? Daddy, it's my birthday tomorrow and ...."

Hearing the unbroken flow of chatter, Maddy marvelled at her daughter's ability to pick up the threads of a relationship she surely could barely remember. But perhaps had continued to practise privately within the confines of that fertile imagination? At last there was quite a long silence, the click of the phone and Bunty came in looking thoughtful.

"All right sweetie?"

She nodded. "I don't think Daddy's coming back."

Maddy knelt down and hugged the small figure tightly. She said "No he isn't," and waited.

"He sounded ... funny."

"They speak a bit differently in Australia."

"Not that sort of funny," Bunty said. She wriggled away. "Oh, bother, I've missed the end of the monkeys." She put on a theatrically wistful expression. "Oh I do *wish* we could have a monkey."

Thank God for a child's resilience.

It was a relief next morning to find her still seemingly unphased by the contact with her father. Indeed she was far too preoccupied with opening presents and cards, and making ever wilder guesses at the nature of that afternoon's promised treat. Her expression when they finally entered the theatre was a joy to see, and she settled into her seat near the front of the stalls, hugging herself with anticipation. Maddy found almost as much pleasure in watching her as in the show, though it was a colourful performance with an excellent cast.

Then, after the second interval, the musicians returned to the orchestra pit and "Look!" shrieked Bunty. "The Perhaps-Angel."

And so it really was, Maddy saw with equal if quieter amazement, observing for the first time the very large harp and the familiar figure beside it. She also observed that Bunty's clear voice had caused a murmur of amusement through the auditorium and an infinitesmal flicker across Stefan's face.

Thankfully, once the curtain had risen Bunty was so absorbed in the show once more that her further outbursts merged with the rest of the audience's reactions. Maddy felt strangely still.

Afterwards they waited for him at the stage door.

"Bunty and I have come to apologise," Maddy said as Stefan emerged, thankfully alone.

"I knew it could only have been you, Golden Girl" he said, squatting down in front of Bunty. He took her hands. "Happy Birthday again. But I think now I must tell you the truth: I am not an angel, not even a 'perhaps' one."

"That's what Daddy said when he rang me yesterday. But then I thought perhaps they don't have angels in Australia?" Bunty looked at him hopefully.

"Her father lives in Australia now," Emmie explained.

"Ah," Stefan said. There was a small pause before he went on, "Not in Australia. Not anywhere where you can *see* them. They're like a lot of things -

happy feelings and liking feelings. You can't *see* them, but it doesn't mean they're not there."

Maddy thought *Gerry wouldn't have left her with that chink of hope. Anyway who really, really knows?* "It means." she said, "that sometimes you have to take things on trust."

And how long since you've put that into practice my girl, she wondered fleetingly.

Time to examine that thought later. In the meanwhile "Would you like to join us for a birthday supper Stefan?" she said.

----oOo----

They had never looked back. They had married a few months later, Bunty had in due course done media studies and worked her way up to being editor of an arts magazine. Maddy and Stefan had a son who eventually decided to travel the world and finally ended up in the Polish community in Canada.

They had done a lot of travelling themselves, too. Stefan proved to be a natural with computers and jetted from one continent to the other sorting out big business IT problems. When retirement began to poke its nose above the horizon, they settled in Donnington in the Midlands where Stefan got a job as handyman at the care home, and Maddy worked part time in the kitchen. Bunty came to see them quite often, now with two-year-old Trixie who was heading towards being the next Perhaps-Angel in Maddy's life. She was also showing every sign of being as precocious as her mother had been, and loved to visit Manorfields where the old people made a great fuss of her, especially the ones who didn't have grandchildren of their own.

THE WRONG TRACK

Trixie was a favourite of Alice. It was this tiny girl who had broken through the vacuum of loneliness that came in the wake of Alice's widowhood. Through Trixie, she had got to know her mother Bunty and her grandmother Maddy, who was a part time carer at Manorfields Care Home. And she had learned the story of Maddy's romance with Stefan, Manorfields' Polish gardener, and once again marvelled at the circumstances that brought people together. And probably none was more haphazard then her own.

Forty years ago, things had been different. Young women - or at least young women like Alice - had not been so assertive. Everyone had thought Brett was a great catch when they married ten years earlier, except for her parents who thought he was a tad too suave, and her friend Moneybags (aka Penny Pound), who thought him potentially overbearing. But Alice was ecstatic. It wasn't just that he was drop-dead handsome, but he was clever too. She couldn't believe her luck. It took a while to realise that he was also incorrigibly ambitious, self centred and manipulative.

One snag had been that as she finished her librarian course he still had two years to go for his computer degree. "Never mind," she said. "I'll be the breadwinner while you finish your studies, then I'll become a homemaker and we'll have babies." They had a quiet wedding, moved into a flat in a Victorian house on the outskirts of town and settled down to married bliss.

Alice took a job at the local library and joined an evening art class. Her tutor, Felix, was a gem and said she was good. She was thrilled when one of her water colours was chosen for the art school exhibition. "Clever girl," murmured Brett when he heard, but he never found time to visit the exhibition. Alice was really sorry when Felix's father fell ill and he had to return to Liverpool, but she persevered with the new tutor's classes when she could.

Brett got a first in computer technology. They celebrated with a fine meal out and Brett said "Now it's your turn to do what you want."

Only it never quite worked out that way. Brett was soon snapped up by an international computing company looking for someone to help them move forward. He made sure they did and quickly rose to greater heights. No babies came along but perhaps it was just as well, for Brett had now entered the world of targets and trade fairs. As well as being a workaholic, he was a perfectionist. He was also frequently away at short notice or brought guests home for dinner at even shorter notice.

The final chapter had opened when, yet again, he had announced at breakfast that important clients were coming to dine that evening. Alice had protested more vehemently than usual.

"For heaven's sake, Al," Brett had been clearly exasperated. "If it's such a problem I'll cancel the arrangement."

She hated it when he abbreviated her name (according to Brett, Alice was retro). In some way it diminished her, and over the years he had become very good at doing this.

"I don't want you to cancel it," she said quietly. "It's just that the local shops aren't exactly geared to provide the ingredients for an exotic meal at short notice. And I recently cleared out the freezer."

Brett was good at being briefly contrite, too. "Sorry, sweetie. It completely went out of my mind until this morning." He brightened. "Tell you what. I'll load the dishwasher while you get ready so that you can get into town early and buy what you need. You could meet up with Fiona – she's a *cordon bleu* isn't she?"

Big deal Alice thought, but aloud she said "Thanks. I'll go and call her."

Alice sometimes wondered at what point Brett's gratitude for her earlier support gave way to taking it for granted. Perhaps it was about the same time that he began finding fault instead. If she protested, he said he was only joking. So what had happened to her sense of humour?

And yet. She had a lovely home, her own car, the wherewithal to have anything she wanted. "So stop whingeing," she thought, as she stop-started her way into town

. "So what's new?" Fiona asked half an hour later as they settled at a window table.

"Well, Brett's bringing unexpected guests home tonight."

"That's not new, dear friend. And you've heard my views on that subject."

"And don't want to hear them again," Alice said quickly. "What I do want is a couple of suggestions for a main course that doesn't take too long to prepare."

By the time they were on their second coffee, she had jotted down three options and already settled on one: braised lamb with flageolet beans and cherry tomatoes.

"You're a star, Fi."

"What about starter and pudding?"

"They're OK. I've got a great starter recipe for baked tomatoes, chilled and served with basil and black

161

olives. And my fruit salads with soured cream are famous throughout the land."

The rest of the day went well. She got all her ingredients quickly, the traffic had eased for the return drive, and preparing Fiona's dish was as easy as she had made it sound. The Armstrongs were delightful and complimented her lavishly on the meal. It was a pity that Brett had to intervene with "Was that one of Fiona's dishes?" then explaining to their guests about 'Al's *cordon bleu* friend'. But she had become all too accustomed to this kind of put-down.

It was soon after that there was a company-wide challenge for ideas to review the international set-up of the corporation. Best suggestions could lead to interviews for new jobs at larger salaries. The deadline was a month ahead. Brett devoted every evening and most week-ends to preparing his. And having completed and checked it, he scrapped it and started all over again. Twice.

When it was eventually completed to his satisfaction two days before the deadline, he printed it off, put it in an eye-catching folder and showed it to Alice. Well, not so much showed it to her as flicked through its pages, as it was 'all rather technical and boring.' She saw pages of coloured graphs, boxes and a lot of well set-out text. It was impressive. It was also right up against the deadline when it needed to be presented to the new head office in London.

The next afternoon his area boss told him he had been chosen to chair a meeting the next day with a major new client.

"But I'm taking my presentation to head office," protested Brett.

"You shouldn't have left it to the last minute. This is important. Get Alice to take it."

162

Brett already had the rail ticket and spent all that evening and much of the night telling her how important it was, and would she please, *please*, not leave it on the train. By the time he had finished she was full of dread. All the same, she went through her wardrobe and hung out her newest trouser suit: soft mushroom with a waft of russet silk at the throat.

There was a hold up for road works, and another while the largest truck she had ever seen backed out of a supermarket. Thank heavens Brett had bought the ticket in advance. She found a parking place, scuttled into the station, up the stairs, across the bridge, down on to the platform, flung herself on to the waiting train and into a window seat just as it began to move off.

"That was close!" The young man opposite her looked up from his laptop and grinned. "Would you like my paper – I've finished with it."

Still breathless, Alice nodded her thanks and opened the paper. It wasn't often she sat down and really read a newspaper and she was soon engrossed in one or two of the stories. Then she looked out of the window. Fields, woods, farms slid passed like an ongoing video. All those lives being played out in what really was England's green and pleasant land. She was aware of a rare sense of freedom and gave a big sigh.

"My goodness, that sounded heartfelt!"

She smiled back at her fellow traveller. "I was just thinking what a green and pleasant land this is."

He glanced out of the window. "I suppose it is."

Alice continued looking out of the window, dozed, looked out again. She glanced at her watch, saw it had stopped. Brett was always chiding her for forgetting to wind it. She glanced across at the young man, still absorbed in the contents of his laptop screen. Eventually she said "I'm sorry to interrupt you, but my

163

watch has stopped. I imagine we must be getting near London by now."

He stared at her in alarm. "I sincerely hope not! I'm going to Liverpool. As for the time, it's nearly half past one. We're due in about half an hour."

Alice choked back panic. Brett would never forgive her. She could almost hear his litany of her shortcomings unfolding. How had it come to this?

Because you let it happen, came a small voice somewhere at the back of her head.

The young man was looking almost as stricken as she felt. "What on earth will you do?"

Alice smiled at his worried face. "It's really kind of you to be concerned, but it will all sort out."

Heaven knows how. Even if she got the next train south, she would never get to head office in time. She checked her wallet. Well, at least she hadn't forgotten her credit card, so could be sure of a comfortable overnight, a return ticket, and perhaps a guided tour of the city.

Come to think of it, she'd never been to Liverpool before. It was supposed to have fine museums and art galleries, not to mention shrines to the Beatles. It would be nice to explore. Perhaps she would give Felix a ring and see if he could do an art gallery with her. And didn't old Moneybags live up here? They hadn't been in touch for ages. She'd check the telephone directory.

It would be nice to take control of her life for a while. Who knows, she might get used to it?

Before anything else, of course, she must call Brett and eat a massive slice of humble pie. Mustn't she?

In fact she hadn't. She had rung Felix who sounded surprisingly pleased to hear from her. They had visited an art gallery, had dinner, been to the theatre, gone to a stately home, met up with Moneybags - and a day stretched into nearly a week. They had also fallen in love. There had been an acrimonious divorce and eventually nearly forty years of marriage to a soul mate during which she had modest success with her water colours and they had travelled the world. Alas no children.

In retirement they had moved to the village of Donnington where Felix had friends, and they'd become involved in a lot of community activities.

"You'll soon be running this place, too," Felix joked when they moved into Manorfields, six months before he died of some mysterious virus.

No amount of community activity would compensate for his loss, but she was by no means the only one coping with loneliness. In some cases, partners had died in their sleep or at their spouse's feet. She couldn't imagine that. Though watching Felix turn from a relatively healthy old man into a corpse in a matter of days hadn't exactly been fun.

Being part of other people's lives helped, too, especially when there was a long term future ahead as in Trixie's case. Then there were weekly involvements with crosswords with the likes of austere Heather and Phillida who weren't austere at all when you dug a little deeper under those protective exteriors.

JUST NINETEEN DAYS

ASTRA

After the accident, Astra was in Manorfields Care Home for several weeks while ribs, a broken leg, sprained wrist and a kaleidoscope of cuts and bruises gradually mended. Jed, whose real name was Jesse, came to see her regularly and between them they slowly pieced together a tale that spanned seventy years or more. It had begun in April, 1945, nineteen days before the end of World War Two. Astra's father had been the pilot of one of a squadron of Typhoons flying over Germany.

Beyond the fringes of memory Astra reached back for echoes of the fun and giggles as she hid in the garden, when Daddy was home on leave, and he pretended not to know where she was. She would remain hidden for ages and ages until, when she was least on her guard, he would swoop down and scoop her up from behind some shrub or wheelbarrow and, holding her high, twirl round and round until she nearly wet her knickers and Mummy came out protesting he would make her sick.

Then one day he did not come looking for her. In the end she went in to find him in the living room reading a newspaper. When she tried to insinuate herself between him and it, he said, "Daddy doesn't want to play at the moment, sweetheart." He had never wanted to play again.

The war ended and still Daddy hadn't cheered up. Once she started at school, it hadn't mattered so much. She had learned to ride a bike, made friends, gone out for long bike rides into the country at week-ends. It was then she had noticed how different things were in other people's homes, other kids' Dads sometimes joining in their games. And yet, and yet. Somewhere on the edge of memory were those echoes of fun: a Dad who had laughed and come looking for her in the garden, and twirled her high in the air.

"Was Dad always so …. so…." She had not been able to find the right word and ended up with "boring?"

Her mother flared,. "No he was not. He used to be the life and soul of every occasion."

"What happened?"

"The war happened. It changed him almost from one day to the next. He won't talk about it."

After she left school, Astra did a secretarial course, got herself a job in Birmingham and moved into a flat with a girl friend. It was on a week-end visit home that she had found her father's war diaries. They were notebooks rather than diaries, scrawled in chronological order in the sort of exercise books they used to have at school. Gerald Braithwaite hadn't written daily but in bursts, starting from the time he joined up just a few days after the outbreak of war. He was already married and Lily was pregnant with her. She read in amazement about the enormous amount of fun they managed to pack in to those early war years. How could they have been so unafraid?

Of course Dad hadn't mentioned any of that in his diary, but he had written about how he felt every time he got back from an operation. He said he felt like God, all powerful and so elated that all he wanted was to go out and do it again.

Whenever he had leave he and Mum would go off into the countryside. As there was no petrol available, they would hitch hike. They had even taken

167

Astra, strapped in a kind of harness on Dad's back, though she couldn't remember that. They had also gone dancing a lot and to one of the three pictures houses in the town. After a while Astra started skipping bits. Until, that is, she got to the entry for nineteen days before the end of the war.

Sometimes you can feel drunk with gratitude at being alive, at having survived, he wrote, and today started as one of those days. Jeffers' Typhoon was ahead of me and four more ahead of that; behind me Bones' brought up the rear. The blue sky pulsated with the sense of victory all around us, the knowledge that at last this horrendous war was approaching its end.

From 3000 feet Germany was like a map below us, its rivers, railways, roads well defined, all of them teeming with life. Everyone was on the move, most of all the Jerries in retreat from all directions, probably desperate to get away from the Commies moving in from the east. The bridges over the Elbe had been blown up, so no joy in that direction. And from the south and west the British Army was pretty well unstoppable now. Soon it will all be over and I'll be on my way home to my dearest wife Lily, and my beloved Astra, nearly three and the prettiest kid in the free world. Soon to be the whole world.

I'd warned Lily she wouldn't thank us for christening her that, but she wouldn't listen. The kid had been conceived in the middle of an air raid when I was home on leave, and the idea of naming her after part of the RAF's motto had become fixed in Lily's head. They say women get funny ideas when they're pregnant.

Then a voice crackled in my ear. A target had been spotted below and we were going in. Ahead of me I saw the Typhoons point earthwards, one after the other, and I followed suit. The noise and the speed and the promise of the future were intoxicating. The earth was approaching, and the network of roads reduced to one, crowded with men, pale blobs of faces turning skywards. I thought we'll show you. I fired my rockets, pulled back the stick heading back into the sky, noticed with surprise that Bones had broken formation and had headed up and away before any of them.

Bones was almost in tears when they joined up for the debriefing. "Didn't you see? That was no retreating army column. That was a straggle of refugees, maybe p.o.ws. Maybe ours."

It was finally confirmed that he was right. It was nineteen days before the war ended and I never forgot those pale blobs of faces turning up towards me.

The next entries of the diary were even more terse. Sometimes just a word: *haunted*. Occasionally there was a scrawled reference to nightmares of pale faces. A longer more coherent entry described how Bones had been hospitalised with a nervous breakdown.

Astra rang her mother. "Did Dad know someone called Bones? Someone in his squadron?"

Lily said straight away, a laugh in her voice, "Yes, a lad called John Bowman. Everyone called him Bones because he was so skinny. Very serious." She paused. "I think he was invalided out with a nervous breakdown. Not sure your father wasn't on the verge of one himself. He was really very odd after the war."

There followed a gap of several weeks in the diary. Then Gerald Braithwaite wrote a long and obviously carefully considered entry. From it Astra understood that the nightmares from which he had suffered were connected with pale blobs representing the faces looking up as the Typhoons hurtled down towards them and let loose their rockets. Each blob

169

seemed to trigger a fresh nightmare peopled by strangers connected with a blob. Gerald, clearly convinced he was going mad, had consulted a doctor who diagnosed him as suffering from post-war trauma. He had prescribed some pills, the equivalent of modern tranquillisers, which blotted out the nightmares but made him feel like a zombie. The doctor suggested a psychiatrist but Dad was of the stiff-upper-lip generation which sorted out its own problems. Finally, in desperation, he tracked down Bones.

Gerald's diary recorded that Bones had seemed remarkably together and quite obdurate in his refusal to discuss that morning nineteen days before the end of the war. He'd been to hell, he said, and was now on his way back. He could only recommend that Gerald did what he had done. It meant psychiatrists. For whatever reason, Gerald couldn't.

The diary ended about a year before her father's accident. Astra consulted her memory focussing on key events in her life when Dad had been around: exam results, job promotions, broken relationships. All she could remember was her mother's chatter to cover her father's silence.

Soon after Astra had found her father's war diaries, she met her first boy friend. She had her first sexual experiences and wondered what all the fuss was about, but it distracted her from her interest in the war which was fast becoming history. Later she had changed jobs and moved in with a young journalist called Roy. It was one Friday when she was at work that Mummy had rung up to say Daddy had had an accident and was in hospital. She had gone straight there to find Daddy in intensive care, all strung up with tubes. He had crashed into a tree and died that weekend. She sat beside him for hours and several

170

times he had squeezed her hand. She found herself wondering whether it had really been an accidenr or whether he had just given up the struggle with the pale blobs of his nightmares. Once he had smiled and whispered "sorry". Then briefly he had looked like the Daddy she remembered from all those years ago.

JED

About the time Astra was coming to terms with her father's death, Jesse Smith was mopping up the last of his gravy with a crust of bread – a habit he had acquired from Knuckles – and leaned back in his chair. He ran his tongue over his teeth, felt in his pocket and got out the small gold-sheathed toothpick his father had given him. Knuckles watched him probing for a moment and then said, "Gawd you don't half have some Nancy ways."

Jesse removed the tooth pick, wiped it carefully on a paper napkin and looked at him. "You said something?"

Knuckles waved a conciliatory hand. "OK Jed, no offence meant."

Jesse grunted, began probing his teeth again. Knuckles couldn't bring himself to call him by his proper name. They had settled for Jed. Jesse didn't mind.

It was a couple of years since the two had met in a bar near Euston Station. Jesse had just got back from several months as a mercenary in a small African republic fighting for a cause he did not understand or much care about. But he was ace at his job and the money was good. He had noticed Knuckles eyeing him for some time and eyeballed him back. After a while Knuckles came over and said, "You looking for a job?"

"Could be."

"I'm looking for someone with a bit of muscle. You look a useful sort of guy. What's your name?"

"Jesse Smith. What's yours?"

Knuckles had stared, started to grin, saw Jesse's expression, thought better of it. "I'll call you Jed," he said. "Most people call me Knuckles." Glancing down at his companion's beefy hands, Jesse could see why.

It was a construction job, good money tough conditions in some remote part of the north. "They're a tough gang," Knuckles added.

"I'm tough," Jesse said. He'd been tough since Pa had taught him to handle bullies at that fancy school. They'd laughed at his name, which was also Pa's after Grandpa's greatest buddy, an American, who died in the First World War's trenches. Then Pa had been shot down, taken prisoner of war and got shot at and killed. Just nineteen days before the effing war ended. Things might have turned out differently if he hadn't.

After a while Jesse became used to being Jed. Pa would have objected strongly but Pa had long since died on some foreign field. Ma, who never really recovered from Pa's death, had become senile and was quietly enclosed in her own little bubble. She would not have noticed if he had called himself Jezabel. He saw her as often as he could; sometimes she recognised him, more often she did not, but seemed happy to invite him in to whatever fantasy she happened to be living at the time.

"You're good with your mum," Knuckles said. "I'd never have the patience."

He had his own old woman, buxom and jolly, Maisie, and their daughter who was almost a younger clone called May. May had taken a fancy to Jed and Knuckles let it be known he would be glad to welcome him into the family. Their lives had become closely

172

linked. Knuckles clearly regarded Jed as his right hand man in all business negotiations since he had 'a way with words' not to mention 'the right accent'.

They had an import-export outfit for a while and in due course moved into the loan business. Knuckles had a small coterie of brawny youngish men on whom he could call at a moment's notice. Jed refused to have anything to do with strong arm tactics, but he was very good at sweet talking customers into increasing their loans.

And then one day Jed was browsing in a charity shop and his eye was caught by the cover of a book showing a picture of a straggling column of prisoners of war. The summary on the back said it was about the great marches many p.o.ws were subjected to towards the end of the war. He bought it for a quid and read it through the night.

The author had researched it by talking to hundreds of survivors from those marches. Jed knew the camp where his father had been, and the date of his death. He read how weary columns of p.o.ws had inched their way first east, then west; how one day they were in two parallel columns and one of these had been mistakenly shot up by Typhoons, and fifty killed.

It was nineteen days before the end of the war. The day Pa died.

It took a while for it to sink in: that Pa's death and the friendly fire were on the same day and that one could have resulted from the other. As the idea took shape, glowing embers of resentment grew to flaming anger. He had looked up to his father, adored him. It was Pa who had taught him how to stand up for himself. With the abrupt removal of his role model he had concentrated on consolidating his ability to be self sufficient. Then came the army. He did well. Some of his peers recognised in him the potential that would make for a good career as a mercenary. They hadn't sussed out that softer side that Pa had stressed was so important to make you a really strong person. And when it became too difficult to opt out of messier assignments, he simply opted out of the mercenaries. It was soon after that he met Knuckles.

And now he learned that the loss of Pa was probably down to some trigger happy moron within days of the end of the war.

The thought began to dominate his days.

"What's up Jed?" Knuckles asked on several occasions.

"Something on my mind."

"Then for Gawd's sake get it off. You're a right Jeremiah. Take May out and give her a good time."

The next time he went to see his mother, he probed gently: how had Pa died in the war. It was one of her more lucid days. "Telegram," she said. "I got a telegram saying he was reported killed. April, 1945." No more than that, he'd asked? "Later," she said. "Later they said it was some place in Germany, though it sounded like Greece."

He started on some research. There was amazing stuff on the internet and he followed leads in the wildest directions. Through the War Graves Commission web site he found that Pa had been re-interred in a big war cemetery in Berlin. The web site for that said that many of those buried had been prisoners of war marched out of the camps as the Russians approached from the east. He wondered why Ma hadn't had Pa brought home, but by then Ma was starting to be odd. He reckoned she had never got over Pa's death either. Further enquiry yielded the information that the original internment had been a

174

mass grave in a place called Gresse. Gresse … sounded like Greece?

He went to the library and went through several atlases until he found the place: in tiny print about 20 miles east of the Elbe, near a place called Lauenburg. Now all he need was to know who.

And then Knuckles had a crisis and it went out of his mind. Several years later Jed had married May and had first a daughter and, two years later, a boy. They called him Jesse despite Knuckles' protests. And then one day, aged eleven, the child demanded to know what had happened to Grandpa.

"He died in the war," Jed told him. But he didn't add it was only nineteen days before it ended.

ASTRA

About this time, Astra's partner Roy was appointed advertising manager of *Mid Shires* monthly. She had told him about Dad and the friendly fire, but after initial interest he expressed the view it was an obsession she had to rein in or she risked becoming a war bore. Only Astra found she couldn't and by the time she was 30 Roy had moved out. She was making him feel claustrophobic, he said, and anyway he wanted to try his luck in London. It was true that Astra's obsession only increased with time. Though she did not have her father's nightmares, she inherited the pale blobs which intruded as soon as her mind was not especially occupied and even sometimes when it was. She did not visualise the strangers connected with each of them, but she tried to imagine them and in what way they had been affected. It seemed you could inherit the sins of your father.

The intrusion of the pale blobs continued to affect her relationships. Roy had left her with the flat

175

and in it she was successively joined by Eric, Bill and Nathan. In between Eric and Bill, she took a posting overseas with V.S.O. for several years working in different schools in a number of locations in Africa. On her return, during Bill's tenure, she wrote a book about her African experiences. It didn't make much money but established her reputation as a practising liberal. It was about then that she glimpsed herself in a shop mirror and noted with a small shock that she had slipped, unawares, into middle age.

Following Bill, Nathan lasted the longest – nearly five years, in fact, - as he had a penchant for 20th century military history and initially an interest in the fate of Astra's Dad. But her pale blobs were not part of history and in due course indulgence gave way to irritation and eventually to his departure. Her mother gave up exhorting that it was high time she settled down. Astra decided she was quite happy on her owny.

In due course she followed many of the same leads as Jed and acquired the same information with the same gaps. Trawling through the list of those buried in the Berlin cemetery she made a list of all those who had died on the relevant date. Some of them came from Canada, Australia or New Zealand, but most were listed as Royal Air Force Reserve.

Usually the name of the parents and wife of each were given, and the town where they lived. Astra made a list of all the wives and then checked the electoral list of the towns concerned. One of them was named Smith which inevitably produced a large number of links. Some had remarried, some moved away, some simply disappeared but she eventually had a list of half a dozen wives and a couple of elderly parents.

It was surprisingly easy to dispose of the wives. Astra's standard opening was "I'm really sorry to

176

trouble you, but I'm trying to trace relatives of a friend who died in World War Two. Name of Jesse Smith."

The usual response was "Sorry I don't know her."

"Not her, him. Jesse was a man."

There was inevitably a pause then a faintest hint of amusement in the concluding "No, I'd certainly remember a man called Jesse. Sorry I can't help."

Which left a couple of elderly parents: a man in his nineties living alone in Oxfordshire and an old woman in a home in Norfolk. The man's home was a cottage near the village of Donnington. Astra checked in at one of the local pubs. A cheery barmaid knew quite a lot about Jimmie Smith. "Comes in like clockwork, two minutes passed six every evening, has a couple of halves, then goes home again."

Astra was waiting for him, watched him for a while exchanging witticisms with a youngster in his seventies. When the other man had gone, she approached him. "Jimmie Smith? I just wondered if you were related to Jesse Smith who died in 1945?"

The old man put his glass down. "Who wants to know?"

"I'm the daughter of a friend of his."

Jimmie Smith grunted. "Jesse was my brother. We never saw eye to eye, but no one deserves to die like that. Amy, his missus never got over it."

Amy Smith, the last name on her list, the old girl in a nursing home.

JED

That day Jed approached his mother's room from the garden entrance. He was in time to see a strange woman come out of the room and disappear down the corridor. A member of staff was seeing to his mother, settling her into her chair with a cup of tea on the table beside her.

"Who was that?" he asked. "That woman who just left?"

"I don't know, dear. She said she'd come to see Mrs. Amy Smith, but I told her that Amy wasn't well enough to see anyone at the moment and she said she would come back another day."

Jed strode back along the hall, down the stairs to reception and demanded to know who the woman was who had visited his mother. The girl scrabbled among the papers on her desk and produced a visiting card: Astra Braithwaite, researcher, he read, and underneath an address near Banbury, Oxfordshire. Astra – what kind of name was that? Wasn't it something to do with the stars? *Per ardua ad astra* Pa's voice suddenly boomed in his head. Of course, the R.A.F. motto. Somehow that seemed to clinch things.

That Spring, Jed suggested they start going for country drives.

"Do we have to go so far?" protested May, as they regularly headed for the M40.

Jed pointed out that the Cotswolds was a beautiful area and the children would love it. Sadly the children were soon bored by picturesque villages, venerable churches and old pubs where they weren't allowed to run about. They weren't even very impressed by the splendours of Blenheim Palace or the fact that Winston Churchill had been born there. But Jesse became very excited by the lake and the flotillas of ducks on it. So Jed did some more research and found the wildlife park at Burford, and some farms open to the public.

Gradually he widened their range until Banbury started appearing on the signposts.

"There's someone around here I want to look up," he told May.

Astra Braithwaite's cottage was on the outskirts of the town in what had no doubt once been a separate village. They parked across a patch of green. After a while Jesse asked impatiently why they were just sitting there?

"Daddy knows someone who lives in that cottage," May explained.

"That lady coming out?" asked Jesse. And as the woman walked briskly away from them, Jed recognised her as the woman who had visited Ma's room. She looked older than he remembered, perhaps ten years his junior.

After that, the family outings dwindled. Maisie said she was too busy, the children expressed no opinion and Jed preferred to go on his own, sometimes parking for long periods outside Astra Braithwaite's house. But how do you approach somebody whose father may have killed yours nineteen days before the end of a war?

----oOo----

It was Astra's neighbour who noticed Jed's car first. She was a noticing sort of person when it came to local happenings.

"Perhaps you are being stalked," the neighbour suggested. But Astra knew she was not the sort of person that anyone would stalk. The car's occupant was a well built, rather good looking man, probably well into his sixties. Once or twice he brought a rather buxom lady and a couple of young children with him. She thought they were his grandchildren until the little boy called him Dad. Usually, though, he was alone. It was very strange

179

One day she saw the same vehicle leaving the pub car park as she was going in.

"Hi Astra," the landlord greeted her. "There was a fellow in just now asking after you. Left his card."

She read 'Jed Smith, import/export', and an address in the Birmingham area. So why hadn't he come knocking on her door?

But there was nothing now to stop her knocking on his. And she knew what she wanted to say. She wanted to say Jed's Dad should never have died; that his death in a way had killed hers. She wanted to get the pale blobs out of her head.

----oOo----

May, taking a breather from her weeding in the front garden, noticed the Audi parked across the road. At the same time she noticed young Jesse surreptitiously letting himself out through the front gate, pushing his bike. He knew damned well he was not allowed to cycle on the main road yet.

"Jesse!" she called, and then more urgently, **"Jesse!"**

The boy was clamped to the i-Pod they had given him for his twelfth birthday. Of course he couldn't hear her, any more than he would hear the traffic coming up behind.

"Jesse! Jesse!!" shrieked May, bringing Jed hurtling out of the house.

Jesse had his bike on the edge of the kerb, had swung one leg over, one foot resting on the offside pedal.

A woman had come out of the Audi, was crossing the road towards them. She started yelling "Jesse", too. Then, as the boy began to move off,

180

oblivious of the white van fast approaching from behind, she hurled herself in front of it, knocking Jesse to the pavement.

In a moment the boy was sobbing in his mother's arms. Assured that he was all right, Jed went to kneel down on the kerb where the woman's head was just visible. The van driver kept saying over and over again "Came from nowhere….didn't stand a chance…."

Her voice was so quiet that he only just distinguished "So sorry about your Dad."

Jed reached down and held her head gently. "You saved my boy. Oh God. It wasn't supposed to happen like this."

She gave a little smile and said something that it was even more difficult to understand. It sounded like "pale blobs" and then "gone". She was probably hallucinating, poor woman. He stayed there, gently holding her head, until the ambulance came.

LOLLIPOP

"Hello, I don't think I've seen you before. I 've been away a couple of weeks"

Philippa looked up from the book she was reading and saw a pleasant looking man, seventyish, leaning heavily on a stick, who had paused by her seat in the gardens of Manorfields Care Home.

"*Go away,*" she said in her head, but aloud she answered "That's probably because I have only been here a few days and I like to keep myself to myself," she said. "Positively anti-social according to my sister Steph."

"That's a shame. We are really quite a nice crowd here despite our sundry shortcomings. I'm Larry, by the way. Larry Roberts." What a nasty irony. Her husband of twenty years had been Robert until the accident that had ended his life. Hers too in any meaningful sense. "If you don't mind me asking, which flat are you in?"

She did mind, but said reluctantly "Fourteen."

"Oh, we're neighbours. So that means your predecessor Beth did go to live with her son after all."

"I've no idea," Philippa said. Nor interest, her tone indicated.

"Well, I hope my cat Lollipop won't intrude on you. She was rather used to popping in to see Beth." Larry began moving away.

"So do I," Philippa muttered at his retreating back. She'd been told that cats, but not dogs were allowed as long as they were kept under control. Well, they'd see about that.

She had agreed to come to Manorfields with the greatest reluctance. It had become clear soon after she returned home from hospital that she could not manage on her own. In the first place she could not get up the stairs and her left arm was almost useless. Steph and her latest partner had brought her bed downstairs, filled the freezer with food, arranged for a home help.

"I'll manage perfectly well. Do stop fussing," Philippa said crossly, but soon found she couldn't.

"Why don't you have a few weeks in that Manorfields place. There's a section of flats which is precisely for people like you recovering from accidents or operations." Tactfully Steph did not add 'getting over bereavement' as well.

"It'll probably be ghastly. I expect everyone will be terribly jolly. And nosey."

"You're impossible, Phil. They'll likely be trying to make the best of a bad job."

So eventually she had agreed. Siobhan, the manager, had come to see her the first evening and told her all about the bingo and scrabble evenings and the occasional outings. Philippa greeted the information in stony silence and Siobhan gave up. To Philippa's relief each flat was well equipped and self contained: living room, bedroom, bathroom, kitchen and a huge glory hole cupboard where she could store her easel where no one could see it. There was no need to speak to a soul if she didn't want to. And succeeded until this Larry man came along.

Their mutual hope that Lollipop would refrain from visiting her soon proved unfounded.   Philippa returned from putting out rubbish one evening to find a tabby cat curled up on her sofa in the living room.

"Go away," she said. That meant she couldn't leave the kitchen window open in future.

Lollipop looked up, blinked her green eyes and began to purr. Even Philippa recognised that this was a pretty cat: a tabby in the softest colours with white feet and a white chest. Soft to the touch, too, she found as she reached out to feel the top of her head. Lollipop purred even more loudly.

"Oh, no you don't," Philippa said.

"Oh dear," Larry said as he opened the door of his flat to the sight of Lollipop dangling ignominiously over Philippa's arm. "I *am* sorry."

Philippa dumped her in the hall. "She'll soon learn there has been a change of ownership."

But Lollipop proved a slow learner. Sometimes it was totally baffling how she found her way, but find her way in she did. Usually Philippa discovered her curled up on the sofa, sometimes perched on the windowsill, looking out as if she owned the place; at others nosing round the flat as though imprinting its every detail on her feline mind. She was an intensely curious cat. Always she greeted Philippa with a blink of her green eyes and started purring. Always Philippa scooped her up and delivered her to her owner who invariably said "Oh dear, I *am* sorry." A couple of times he invited her in for coffee but after a couple of brusque responses, gave up. Once Larry rang her bell to remind her there was an outing that afternoon to a local stately home.

"Good Lord, not at all my sort of thing," Philippa said. "Anyway I'm in the middle of something."

What she was in the middle of was touching up one of the many water colours she had done while she and Robert were in Africa. They were to go with the memoirs he had written. Africa was where they had spent most of their married life, teaching in remote places, loving the place and the people. Coming back to the UK had been a terrible shock: the values, the self indulgence. They had been back a year, were just beginning to settle in to rural middle England when the accident ended Robert's life and smashed hers. No time even to say goodbye,

Steph had always marvelled at their silent relationship which had been built on mutual interests and companionship. All the time they were in Africa she had done the water colours, mostly of people, colourfully dressed, doing the sort of things people in Africa do. It was Steph who had slipped the easel into the back of her estate car along with the bulging portfolio of water colours. When at last she got around to looking at them, there were details that cried out for attention. Some were even mere sketches waiting to be finished off. It was strangely therapeutic, reliving those purposeful years; and brought Robert closer.

Steph arrived a couple of times when she was working on them, but tactfully said nothing. The second time, though, she ventured 'those are really good. You ought to have an exhibition.' She also brought Philippa a book of yoga exercises 'to beef up your muscles a bit.' They were oddly pleasurable to do and whether or not she beefed up any muscles, she could certainly manage steps better and even began to get some action from her useless left arm.

Once Steph said, "Have you had your hearing checked lately, Phil? I rang the bell three times before you heard."

"Had the radio on," Philippa said. A small lie seemed better than an argument.

On another occasion Steph commented "By the way Phil I got talking to the guy in No. 16 – Larry I think his name is. Pleasant chap."

"I do wish you wouldn't call me Phil," Philippa said. "Yes, Larry's OK, if a bit on the nosey side." And Steph had shrugged and gone on her way.

185

Philippa became totally absorbed in the water colours, completing the unfinished ones, tinkering with the others until she was satisfied. Coming to them fresh so long after she had painted them, she began to see some merit in them herself. She spent days at a time in the flat only going out for shopping. There was no sign of Lollipop. From time to time she saw Larry in the distance, but the next time she had a closer encounter she hardly recognised him. He seemed to have shrivelled into himself, aged ten years or more.

"Is Mr Roberts unwell?" she asked of Siobhan.

"He will be if he goes on like this. No, he's lost his cat."

How absurd to be so affected by the disappearance of an animal, Philippa thought. All the same she did a tour of her flat, feeling slightly ridiculous as she called "Lollipop, Lollipop….." But there was no response. When she went to the shops again, she saw a notice on the wall asking if anyone had seen the animal, and a rather smudgy photograph of it. The same notice was in the newsagents.

"I'm planning on going home soon," she told Steph on her next visit.

"Yes, I reckon you're about ready," her sister agreed,

Siobhan agreed, too, and they settled on the end of the month. It was then that Philippa began to panic. She was normally a methodical person and was suddenly aware of the chaos that seemed to surround her: notes on her water colours written at the time she had first begun them but now separated from their final versions, scrawled comments on details she needed to check. In the middle of the night she remembered that she had kept a detailed log of every sketch and its progress, not only the precise location and events connected with it, but their progress over the years. Would Steph have recognised the importance of all those scraps of paper in rather higgledy piggledy lack of order stuffed into a file?

By two o'clock she knew she would not sleep and got out of bed. There was no light in the glory hole cupboard, so she took a torch and gave an exclamation of relief as she recognised the bulky file propped up amongst some books. She was about to back out when her bare foot touched something soft. She focussed the torchlight downwards and the next minute was on her knees.

Lollipop.

Limp but not quite lifeless, the cat lay by the door of the glory hole. It was a miracle she had not trodden on her when she came in. Lollipop made an infinitesmal movement, opened her mouth, but no sound came out.

Philippa hurried into the kitchen to find a bowl, poured a little milk into it, went into the bathroom and found an eyedrop dispenser she had bought and never used. Then she carried Lollipop's limp form into her bedroom and stroked her very gently. Finally there came the softest rumble.

"Oh Lollipop," Philippa said. "You must have cried out and I didn't hear."

Very gently she massaged the animal's throat as she cajoled her into taking in milk drop by drop, marvelling at the cat's resilience as she began to absorb it more and more quickly. And then at once Lollipop had had enough, put her head back on the bed and fell asleep. Very quietly, Philippa slid back into bed without disturbing her. Hopefully she would not look such a forlorn creature by the time she was returned to her owner. And then she found she was crying herself:

not just for the cat, but for all the grief she had not managed to express before and for her own self-imposed isolation.

She awoke to something soft poking into her neck. As she remembered the events of the night and sat up, it was amazing to see Lollipop, still thin and wobbly, but showing an unmistakable interest in life. There was a pool of damp on the bed cover. Philippa stripped the bed clothing off and went in search of more milk. Lollipop's purring was now quite prodigious as she alternately lapped the milk and wound round Philippa's legs as she dressed. Then she wrapped her in a small shawl and went to No. 16.

It was 7.30 a.m. She heard Larry muttering grumpily as he came to the door. Then he opened it, saw Lollipop and burst into tears.

"I'll make some tea," Philippa said. It was what you did when anyone was in shock.

When she brought it through to the living room, Lollipop and Larry were looking at each other adoringly. Then Lollipop looked at Philippa, blinked her green eyes and purred.

"She likes you," Larry said.

Philippa said gruffly "She'll have to get used to someone else soon. I'm leaving at the end of the month."

"Oh. Oh, that's a shame. I'll quite miss you Pippa." Larry smiled. "Even though you're a bit of a curmudgeon. I was rather hoping you'd come on the next outing to Frensham so that I could show you where I lived before we went to India."

"I didn't know you'd lived in India."

"You haven't given me much chance to tell you."

"I might well. Come on the outing I mean," Philippa said, aware that she hadn't really minded being called Pippa. She stood up. "I'll leave you both to it. Come over for a coffee this evening. With Lollipop if you like."

"I'll do that," Larry said.

Lollipop simply blinked her green eyes and purred.

RAGBAG

Mother has suddenly started looking frail. Sitting in one of the armchairs in her room at Manorfields Care Home, I watch her breathing, a bit shallow, and smile at the quiet rhythmic snore. At one moment her eyes flicker open and she murmurs "Olivia," before falling asleep again. She's asleep more often than not when I visit these days, so there's plenty of time to think how little I knew her - *really* knew her. And wonder how many people ever did.

Well, of course those who shared her beliefs knew her - the ones who have provided a steady trickle of visitors since she has been here and taught me a lot about her. And then there's my brother Shane, though he has never been a great talker. But as for Father, who died a few years ago, he and mother could not have been more different. Attraction of opposites I suppose.

Once I asked him what had been the attraction and he'd laughed and said, "Quite simply because she was so funny and unpredictable and I never knew what she'd pull out from that ragbag of a mind of hers, my darling bubby Lou."

For father that was quite a statement. He did not go in for "sentimental twaddle". I'm told he and I are very alike, which could have something to do with the fact that I never married. Not that I mind. I have a life I wouldn't swap for anything, involved in environment issues at an international level, jetting about to conferences that hopefully may stop, or at least slow down our self-destruct. That's the bit I did inherit from Mother: preoccupation with the welfare of the environment. Shane has inherited it too, but he's a young male version of Mother and believes in protests and demonstrations rather than politics and negotiation.

That was how they met, my parents, at a demonstration. Well, to be accurate, Mother was demonstrating and Father was on the receiving end as he was then a local councillor and the demonstration was against a new road destroying a bit of woodland. Mother was spokesperson for the group and Father was enchanted by her enthusiasm and gamine looks which were very fashionable at the time.

That was during her Green Period, Father explained, which went on for rather a long time: through their courtship, the first couple of years of their marriage and Mother's pregnancy with Shane. The pregnancy-time protest was when she sat under an oak tree for two days to stop them pulling it down for road widening. She wasn't the only one, of course; there were plenty of others, but none as visibly pregnant as she was. "You oughta be looking after yourself, Mother," the genial cop said apparently as he hauled her up under the armpits. "Leave this sort of thing to those with nothing better to do."

Father had pointed out that if they didn't widen the road there'd be more obstruction and frustration (it was long before road rage) which would eventually affect the local economy, people's jobs, health. Reason won of course and Mother is reported to have howled like a banshee as she watched the oak tree come down. Shane was born two weeks later. And like Mother, he's full of vision of how the world should be, but not much clue about how to make it happen.

Initially she was more into the environment than human rights, but that changed, too. Vietnam all but passed her by until they published that photograph of the kids running down the street towards the camera,

191

one of them naked, her mouth wide open and you could almost hear the screams coming out of the picture. They'd dropped napalm bombs on some village.

"They were aiming at the rebels," Father explained when I raised it with him, but for once even he sounded uncertain.

So Mother became anti-war and, in due course, anti-nuclear – not in any major capacity of course – just one of the faithful crowd trying to ease its sense of helpless outrage. Shane went with her, initially in a push chair, then toddling along with his mini banner. He loved it: the fuss everyone made of him, partly because he was blonde and very beautiful; and he had enormous fun with all the other kids.

Father went on patiently explaining why there had to be wars (to sort out all the baddies) and nuclear power (to provide us all with the things we had come to take for granted); but he also went on providing sandwiches and coffee and, now, fizzy drinks for Shane. He (Father that is) put his foot down when Mother started thinking aloud about joining a peace camp outside a nearby army barracks. Apparently she didn't push it as by then she was expecting me and having all-day morning sickness for a while.

And, of course I proved completely to be my father's daughter, which must have been a terrible disappointment to Mother. Whereas she and Shane lived their lives almost entirely by instinct, from a very early age I was planning my every move with great thought as to its outcome. I learned much earlier than Shane at precisely which point a tantrum could work in my favour or become counter productive. And I think it's fair to say I could twist my steady, unflappable, straight thinking father into a corkscrew.

By the time I started secondary school, Mother was becoming an embarrassment. It's really not funny to see your mother regularly in the local paper in the photographic forefront of some demonstration. After I had protested several times to Father, he said resignedly. "You have to accept she's different from us, Olivia. You see, we like to work things out, understand the reasons for things. Your mother – and your brother come to that – go in more for feelings, need to express themselves in other ways, like joining protests. And it doesn't really do any harm."

After that I tried to be a bit more understanding. Of course it probably helped that some of my more misguided school mates apparently thought Mother was Really Cool.

I missed Shane dreadfully when he went off to College. Of course, he'd moved on in other ways too. Not least he was dating girls and had acquired a painful taste in jungle music. He graduated, if that's the right word, from ponytail to dreadlocks to shoulder length hair and designer stubble, which I think looks quite bizarre but seems to pull the girls in. The first girl was a disaster of Barbie Doll proportions, but thank God his hormones have gradually become more selective and he eventually settled for one of the Green Wellie brigade called Fiona, known as Fifi by everyone except me. She has just produced my first niece.

There was a time when Mother started calling me Ollie, but I soon put a stop to that. Sometimes I caught her looking at me in a puzzled way. She was probably convinced that I'd never produce anything as cuddly and messy as a baby, and indeed I haven't.

Anyway, all the while Father shunted steadily up his career ladder to become something important in banking. In recent years this involved him in quite a lot

193

of travel to international seminars and conferences and workshops. When he was away, Mother sometimes became quite audacious and even occasionally landed up in a police cell for a few hours. In Father's absence this left me feeling terribly responsible. "Ah, you again," was the usual police reaction once they'd got to sorting them out, and they'd ring home and I'd go and pick her up. I only once tried to sit her down for a Serious Talk, but I might as well have been talking to myself.

"I hate the thought of you mixing with those sort of people, Mother. Layabouts with nothing better to do than stir up trouble. I mean what *is* the point?" She explained patiently that the people I was describing were just the fringe lot, the small minority who get all the publicity because who wants to see pictures of thousands of ordinary people holding hands or just walking silently. So I tried a different tack and said, "I know you feel strongly about these things, and I do admire you for it. But wouldn't it be just as effective if you all wrote letters?"

I then got an even more patient speech about how she'd done the letter-writing bit and could paper a couple of walls with the bland replies from every imaginable government department. But I think the fact was that she'd got a bit addicted to the action. And the camaraderie.

At some point there were the Falklands, followed by nasty happenings in Africa and in due course the Iraq invasion of Kuwait. And then along came the Balkans. For several years during the 1980s, we'd had some fantastic holidays, the four of us, in Yugoslavia as it was then. Mostly on the Dalmatian coast around Dubrovnik and on the island of Korčula. That period was probably the nearest that our parents

194

got to being a normal, still-youngish couple enjoying an annual break with the kids. We loved the freedom of it – Shane spending hours exploring the rocky coastline and meeting up with his Yugoslav peers who dressed and talked just the same as he did; and listened to the same jungle music. And I got in with a chess playing group in a local *kafana*. Yes, truly. They play a lot of chess in Yugoslavia. Or former Yugoslavia, as they call it now.

We took inland trips to Mostar and Sarajevo, and once did a coach trip to the medieval monasteries in south Serbia. Of course at that stage I hadn't a clue that Dalmatia belonged to Croatia, that Kosovo was just a part of south Serbia, that Sarajevo was in a sort of melting pot of history and culture called Bosnia. So when it all started falling apart I thought of those great guides and friendly waiters and innumerable kindnesses from strangers and wondered for the first time whether they were Croats or Serbs or Bosniaks. And why did it suddenly matter?

It was terrible to watch the news pictures of torched churches or mosques, devastated villages, lines of Serb refugees leaving Croatia, Muslims leaving Serb areas, Croats leaving etc., etc. Mother ran coffee mornings and jumble sales and collected like mad for the International Red Cross and left them to sort out who needed what the most.

And then came Kosovo. And the NATO bombing.

Mother was enraged. Father explained, "But of course we had to do something. For heaven's sake sweetie, you *saw* those endless refugees, heard their stories."

To which Mother's response was, "And how is bombing a whole lot of innocent people going to help another lot of innocent people? Or how will it stop the spreading spiral of tit for tat violence? Do you really think They knew what They were doing." And I did think she had a point.

And then came 9/11, our involvement in Afghanistan and the Iraq war. Of course Mother was among the million or two who took to the streets against the invasion of Iraq. And even though it patently didn't make any difference, it didn't stop Mother heading for the next major G7 conference, where there was to be an outcry against the huge sums certain bankers and industrialists were awarding themselves in relation to the growing number of food banks sprouting up round the country.

The rest I learned from one of her co-protesters, though we'd seen the newsreels so it was no great surprise to find mother in a clinic with several stitches in her head, a black eye and bruised ribs. The co-protester explained that particular copper didn't pause to ask if Mother were anyone's grandmother while he held her in an armlock.

Mother's enthusiasm for saving the world seemed to wane rather after that. Or perhaps it was to do with Father's illness which merged into dementia and demanded much more patience than I could muster. Perhaps it was all that standing around and waiting, but Mother seemed to have just the level of intuition which allowed for his short term memory loss, but acknowledged the existence of the person he had once been and could still sometimes be again. And so in recent times I have developed a rather different outlook on what Father once called 'the ragbag' of Mother's mind. I've come to appreciate that out of a ragbag you can produce a rich and beautiful quilt.

After he had died, she downsized from house to compact flat but stayed in Donnington where she knew so many people. including a few that she visited regularly in Manorfields Care Home. So it made sense that in due course she should move in there herself.

Mother's eyes flickered open. She mumbled, "What …? I must have dozed off. Sorry, Ollie."

And these days I don't dream of correcting her.

A MORE DISTANT HORIZON

Zoe was incurably and unashamedly a romantic. It had got her into a lot of trouble in her younger years until she tried becoming more hard-wired and that had not proved any better. She was also a good listener and, since she and Whizz had moved into Manorfields Care Home a couple of years back, she had set aside listening time for fellow residents, nearly all of whom were living proof that fact is stranger than fiction.

"Your life is one big cliché," Whizz told her occasionally, usually accompanied by a hug that said *and I love you for it.*

Whizz had discovered listening skills, too - in particular since he heard of the fast one Harry Briggs had pulled over those cheeky Carson twins. He and Harry had taken to regular pints over at The Horseshoe on Tuesday, Thursday and Sunday evenings during which they put the world to rights. While he was out Zoe did some listening or indulged in daydreaming. And then, as often as not, she was back forty years and far away in perhaps the darkest moments of her life.

In fact, she would be back in Nepal among the marbled spaces of Kathmandu's nearly-best hotel, glimpsing her reflection amongst an acreage of polished glass. Even now she could visualise her then slim figure relaxed in stylish pant-suit, long soft mink coloured hair to her shoulders ….

"I love your hair," Chris had often said. "Promise you'll never cut it Zo."

She had promised, of course, but presumably since there was no more Chris – at least not in *her* life – it wasn't really binding any more. Perhaps she'd cut it when she was forty at which life was said to begin. In two years. Twenty-one months to be precise.

"Excuse?" Zoe looked up at the young Nepalese receptionist. "Missis Smithson?"

"No, sorry." She smiled. The young Nepalese were, almost without exception, beautiful and graceful and made you feel like smiling. As he turned away she continued conversationally, but only in her head, *Actually I'm Zoe Rivers. Until recently co-habiting with Chris Gray. But apparently we knew each other too long and too well. Like comfortable old shoes. And who wants to go on living with a comfortable old shoe? Well, I did actually. But Chris didn't, and that's why I'm sitting here like the only unripe cherry in the bowl.* She grimaced at this last vision and from two sofas away a man smiled back. *Oh Lord. You're losing it, woman.* Zoe got up hastily and headed for the door.

Finding a seat in the hotel's magnificent gardens, she lifted her head to the sun and closed her eyes against a blaze of bougainvillea. It was much the same colour as Chris's shirt the day he'd announced, "I don't know how to say this," and then proceeded to do so very fast, as if long rehearsed. He'd realised suddenly (suddenly? after four steady years?) they weren't right for each other. He still loved her, always would, like a friend but not as a lover. He was desperate with regret but it was better to face the fact now than later, etc., etc.

"How suddenly?" she had interrupted, but quite calm. The eye of the storm.

That bit hadn't been rehearsed. It came out in jerks and pauses, but the crux of it was that they knew each other too well. And, by the way, there was someone else.

"You can have the flat," he said to fill the silence she left to hang between them.

"I don't want the bloody flat," said Zoe, who never usually swore. She'd moved briefly in with Viv, her partner in a small travel agency; then found her own place.

It was like bobbing about in a vacuum: an alien landscape devoid of all the familiar signposts she had so carefully built up to overcome her own insecurities.

"You're a real natural at sorting out what people want," Viv had always said.

Yes, but it was her own needs that had always left her deeply uncertain until the advent of Chris. He was one of their regular business clients: a successful young architect.

"I want to look after you Zo," he said over and over again, and she had come totally to believe it.

"You look ghastly," Viv told her a month after she had moved out. "There's a special promotion to Nepal. We could do with an update."

----oOo----

From the moment she arrived, the whole exotic, ramshackle strangeness of Kathmandu had catapulted her back into reality. Here was a place that didn't allow for vacuums.

"Mind if I join you?"

"What?" Zoe opened her eyes.

"Sorry I'm probably pushing my luck." The pleasant craggy face of the man who had smiled at her managed to look at once wry and hopeful. "It's just that I'm here for a few days after a Conference in Delhi. A bit tired of my own company. Just wondered if I could join you."

"I'd rather you didn't." *Oh dear!* "Sorry that was really rude. It isn't you, it's anyone. I'm a bit anti-people just now."

"Right." He hovered a moment more. "Maybe see you later."

Not if she could help it. She had only just begun cautiously to appreciate the unfamiliar freedom of her own company; to stay as little or linger as long as she liked before the extravaganza of carvings on a Hindu temple or the impenetrable serenity of a statue of Buddha. Firmly she fished the guide book from her bag.

It was sunny but still cool as she stepped down from her cycle rickshaw next morning and glanced up at Swayambhunath Buddhist Temple on its hilltop perch to the west of the city.

"I will be your guide. I make good price for you." Zoe disposed of the young man with a confident, well practised "No need thank you, I'm a guide myself." Which was true, if only a self-guide. You learned quickly when you discovered you'd paid three times over the odds for a taxi ride or a pendant or a prayer wheel.

Strangely she found she didn't mind. These people with their magnificent dark eyes and ready smiles made her feel curiously at home. Anyway they too had a living to make. After her initial mistakes she began to enjoy the bargaining game, found she was good at it, appreciated the mutual satisfaction of a fair price reached.

Chris would have been surprised.

The steps up to the temple were covered with stalls heaped with souvenirs. As she paused for breath a beautiful girl by a table piled with woven shawls lifted one and let it cascade over her arm. Threads of gold glinted among glowing sunset colours. "How much you give?"

Zoe smiled, shook her head.

"OK. Not buy. Cost nothing to look." She held it out.

"It's lovely." It would look spectacular with that black top Chris had always liked so much. *Damn you Chris. Go away.*

"How much you give? Any price you like."

"I don't want it. Really."

They bartered amiably and settled on the equivalent of a fiver. The beautiful face shone with pleasure. Zoe thought *I don't need it, but I love it and it's worth the money to see that smile.*

A figure fell into step beside her. "That was an impressive bit of bargaining," said the man from the hotel. "Is this an anti-people day by the way?"

"It's the small talk I can't handle."

"Only the greatest utterings will pass my lips," he promised. "Other than to introduce myself. Michael Pierce."

"Zoe Rivers."

He kept his word. They reached the top of the steps and explored unhurriedly and almost in silence the complex of temples, statues, symbols grouped round the great central stupa. A group of school girls in neat blue skirts and blazers and crisp white blouses chattered over a table of trinkets.

Zoe said "Wouldn't they put most of our school kids to shame?" It made a pleasant change to have someone with whom to share an observation.

"I was thinking much the same."

"When I was that age …" Zoe stopped.

He said sternly "Unfinished sentences are not part of the agreement."

She laughed. "Something I haven't thought of for years. Would you believe my parents were seriously into flower power? I truly thought the whole adult world wore trailing skirts and sandals and dripped with beads. You can't imagine the relief when an unexpected Auntie Winifred whipped me away to a little school where we all wore red cardigans, blue skirts and white blouses. I must have been the only little girl who polished her shoes every day." Zoe paused. She couldn't remember telling anyone that before.

"A child who found relief in a structured life."

"Are you a child psychologist?"

"I taught for a while so I know a bit about kids. Now I'm in I.T,."

"I.T.? Oh Information Technology."

He nodded. "Hence the conference in Delhi."

As they retraced their steps the hubbub of the bazaar rose to meet them. They found themselves outside a small shack framed by cascades of mango, pineapple, citrus fruits.

"So what happened to Auntie Winifred and the flower-power parents?" Michael asked as an enormous jug of freshly squeezed mango juice was put before them.

"Aunt Winifred remains the sanest person in my life. My parents joined a commune somewhere in America from which I get an occasional whacky missive." She looked at him thoughtfully. "Since small talk seems to flourish on mango juice, it's your turn now."

He shrugged. "There's no way I can compete. Average at everything until I found maths. Then it was computers with which I became, as my ex-wife regularly put it, totally obsessed."

Ah. Ex-wife.

Michael looked across at her "And you?"

"Computers? Oh, I can take them or leave them."

He said "You know I didn't mean that."

"OK, I have an 'ex' too." No need to go into detail.

"Some people don't know when they're well off." He grimaced. "Ouch, that was wildly naff, and I thought I was doing so well."

Zoe raised an eyebrow. "Well at what?"

"At not being naff I suppose." He caught her flicker of a grin and went on accusingly "You're winding me up."

"Just a bit." Zoe couldn't remember winding anyone up before.

After that it didn't seem at all odd that they should arrange to share a taxi the next day to visit the Golden Temple and pottery market at Bhaktapur; followed by an evening of Nepali music and dancing in the Thamel quarter. And there was only a twinge of hesitation when Michael proposed a two-day trip to Nagarkot for a sunrise view of the Himalayas.

He kept to his word, steering clear of all the personal stuff, though Zoe gleaned he lived in York, his wife had 'gone walkabout with someone else' and they were childless. In time they found they shared similar preferences in books and theatre, and wrangled amiably over differences in musical and sporting tastes. He confessed to being a couch potato, but was hopefully prepared to be reformed.

"I'm not in the business of reformation," Zoe said.

Michael grimaced. "Still haven't quite got the hang of it, have I?" he said, looking so theatrically dejected that she had to laugh.

And there *was* a great deal of laughing: of the kind of absurd slightly surreal fun she and Chris had once shared and which had trickled away so insidiously she had not noticed it go. As for those sunrise moments over the white turrets of the Himalayas, as the sky went through sensational transitions of light and colour, Zoe knew these would be forever defining moments in her life. Almost an affirmation of her being. She was grateful for Michael's silence.

He was due to leave two days before her. He chose a garden restaurant near the hotel for their farewell supper. She knew she was going to miss him, but she hadn't actually meant to say so as they strolled hand in hand back to the hotel.

Michael stopped, his eagerness palpable. "You must know how much I want to go on seeing you."

"I'm not about to dematerialise," Zoe said lightly.

"I'm serious Zoe. I know you're wary of another relationship. Me too. But it's been a fabulous few days. Just as I wanted it to be."

Somewhere in the deepest recesses of Zoe's mind a small warning bell sounded. *Just as I wanted it to be?* Michael raised her hand to his lips. It felt good. He said "There's nothing I'd like more than to look after you Zo."

The warning bell sounded louder. Almost Chris's very words. She had wallowed in the security of them, almost unconsciously geared her life to his, learned to want the same things, become partner and helpmeet in every sense. And ended up a comfortable, discarded old shoe.

"Just think about it Zoe. And I'll call you when you get back." He was smiling, confident. "Though I'll need your number first."

Yes, he would, wouldn't he? Zoe drew her hand gently away. "You're right – it's been a wonderful few days. And, right again, I *am* wary of relationships. I'm only just beginning to understand that looking-after needs to be a two-way business, and only just discovering that I quite like looking after me. I need time Michael. Probably quite a lot of it. So how about giving me your number, and I'll ring you?"

She had taken his number, lost it, found it and lost it again. And had been surprised at how dismayed she was at losing it. When she found it the second time, she wrote it down in several places and then, almost without thinking, rang it.

"*Whizz-oh!*" exclaimed Michael.

"You sound like Bertie Wooster," Zoe said and giggled. Then he had laughed and they arranged to meet and had picked up where they had left off.

They had had a wonderful forty years of companionship, which continued to survive the creaking limbs and decreasing mobility which had brought them to Manorfields. She only called him Whizz when they were alone; after all, not everyone would think it a suitable name for an eighty-plus-year-old.

SISTERS

Hospital treatment had come to pick Margaret up for her Wednesday physiotherapy session soon after breakfast. Lorna waved her off, as usual, from Manorfields Care Home car park. She always missed her on physiotherapy days. As she turned back into the home, she smiled wryly. It hadn't always been like that.

In fact, as children, they were inseparable: Lorna, steady, a tad solid; Margaret, eighteen months younger, slim, outgoing. By the age of ten Margaret had rechristened herself Maggi and decided she was going to work in television. She was also the leader on adventures and scrapes for which Lorna usually got caught, and, therefore, the blame. Disarmingly, Maggi would assure everyone it was really *her* fault: so disarmingly that they were both forgiven.

In their teens, Maggi became a shiny-haired blonde, Lorna remained a slightly unmanageable bouffant brown. It was at this time they also went on a holiday exchange abroad, Lorna to a small town in Normandy where she became hooked on cooking, and Maggi to Hamburg where she learned to hone her dress sense and her extroversion. They remained close, but began to socialise in different circles.

"You're getting boring," Maggi told Lorna when she opted to stay at home and try new recipes instead of joining her sister at a party.

By late teens, Maggi had a string of boyfriends; Lorna had one, Bob, as steady as she was. They married at twenty, had a son and twin girls by twenty-five. By then Maggi was world-travelling as a rising star with a fashion firm in London. Lorna missed her, though Maggi regularly visited to share her joy or sorrow about her latest man, or most recent professional move. And 'to extract you from the awful rut you're in'. Then Maggi fell in love and moved in with someone called James who was something to do with television.

Later, she became an overnight star in a sitcom called *Paradise Found* and vanished on location in Spain for weeks at a time. Once she invited Lorna and Bob to join her, but it was not a great success. Lorna got the distinct feeling that her sister felt ill at ease with her family's down to earth ways by comparison with the brisk, bright interchanges between her fellow members of the cast and the production team.

After that Lorna and Bob kept to their favourite haunts in Normandy where Bob interviewed the more aged locals and tramped the World War Two beaches for the talks he now gave all over the county. It was his way, he said, of honouring his Dad who had died on those beaches. And while he researched, Lorna expanded her culinary skills.

The family and a growing circle of friends who sampled the results of these skills agreed that Lorna was good enough to be on the telly. Especially for her pâtés which may have originated in Normandy recipes but which Lorna adapted with a new herb here and drizzle of different flavouring there. "Certainly good enough to sell on the local market," Jane, her neighbour and best friend proclaimed persistently.

Lorna started a small stall really to keep her quiet, and sold out in the first hour of the first market morning. She doubled the quantity for the second week and, by the end of a couple of months, was protesting that she was now producing on an industrial scale.

"Yummy. Delicious," Maggi said when she blew in unexpectedly one week-end. That was the week-end she also said, "I don't think Mother should be living on her own much longer. She's going a bit funny."

"Funny?"

"You know, forgetting things, getting confused."

The crisis came sooner than either of them expected when Mother fell and was found by a neighbour.

"The trouble is," Maggi said, "I can't do much with all my travelling." She put on what Bob called her 'lost spaniel look', but Lorna had already interpreted correctly that, when it came to the nitty-gritty, Maggi was expecting her to look after Mum.

By then the twins had married and Bob Junior was doing something incomprehensible in the EU so they had plenty of room. Maggi, delighted to be relieved of any responsibility, assuaged her guilt by agreeing to fund a 'granny annexe' out of the conservatory that Lorna and Bob had long been planning to reconstruct. In the meantime, Mum settled into Bob Junior's room appearing for meals and, when she could be persuaded, into the living room.

"She gives me the willies," Bob Senior muttered regularly.

"She's ill, love," Lorna said defensively, but had to agree that the sight of Mum staring gloomily into space for hours on end was not likely to brighten anyone's day.

It was Mum herself who unwittingly provided the solution. Lorna found her one morning obsessively reducing a piece of toast into ever-smaller crumbs. Aware of Lorna watching, she looked up with a smile that transformed her face. "These are for your recipes," she said.

"She looked twenty years younger," Lorna told Bob that evening.

"Well, if that's all it takes, why not get her on to your own herbs?"

Lorna beamed at him. "You're a genius."

With the growth of demand and increasing preoccupations at home, she had been obliged to cut a few corners, notably using dried rather than freshly ground herbs and spices. Mum, along with a few culinary tools, provided the perfect answer. Of course she needed supervision, otherwise there would be a surplus mountain of sage and a total dearth of paprika, but it was a small enough chore in return for a continuous supply of fresh flavourings and a rejuvenated Mum.

Then she announced she wanted to come to the market, too. "She'll wander off and get lost," Bob warned. "Or put the customers off with her babble."

He was wrong. Mum did not budge from the stall and her smile was a magnet for older customers. "My daughter, my daughter," she informed them, waving an all-embracing arm over the display of pâtés. And that was how she greeted the young reporter from the local paper.

Lorna and Mum are the stars of the market the reporter wrote in the following week's issue, and there they both were, Mum waving and grinning, and Lorna serving a queue of customers. Following the newspaper report there was a flurry of new customers. One Lorna noticed in particular: a tall man, clever-looking, who tried a new pâté each week. On the fourth week he bought a very large portion indeed of the one she called *citronade..*

"So you have settled on this one?" she couldn't help commenting.

"It was a hard choice but this one's a real winner. And I guess there's more than lemon in it."

Lorna grinned. "The other ingredients are mine to know and yours to guess."

"Fair enough." He took the packet she handed him and added surprisingly, "I'm Christopher Brent by the way."

"Glad to meet you Christopher Brent."

Regional television were on the phone soon after. They were doing a series on older people and their problems, they said. Lorna and Mum would fit in splendidly on one they were doing on coping with mental decline. The producer was called Christopher Brent.

""Well I'll be darned," Lorna said. "At this rate I'll have to give up the day job."

"What needs darning, dear?" Mum asked.

"Never mind, Mum."

Towards the end of market morning on the eve of their meeting with Christopher Brent Mum suddenly called out "Maggi!". She was always getting their names mixed up even though they hadn't seen Maggi for months, so Lorna, in the middle of serving a queue of people, automatically responded "Yes, Mum?"

"Maggi!" repeated Mum with a note of defiance. Lorna finished dealing with one customer and turned to her mother before dealing with the next. The old lady was sitting quietly in her usual chair, elbows on the table, a beaming smile on her face, as she looked up at a younger woman leaning across towards her.

"Maggi?" Lorna said, then more certainly "Maggi! Where on earth have you sprung from?"

Her initial hesitation was justified. Apart from the unexpectedness of her presence, Maggi had changed dramatically. Uncharacteristically her hair was dishevelled. She looked as though she had not had a good night's sleep for rather a long time, and bereft of make up her face looked tired and - yes, old.

"I met Christopher in the canteen and he told me about your programme," Maggi said, and burst into tears.

"Christopher?" queried Mum.

"Christopher Brent. Producer of our programme," Lorna said over her shoulder. "Hang on Mags, I'll be there in a mo."

Mum smiled beatifically. "Oh *that* Christopher. Such a lovely young man." She reached out and patted Maggi's hand. "Don't cry darling. Lorna will sort it all out."

Hearing her, Lorna smiled to herself. Yes, she supposed she had become quite a good sorter-outer in her middle years. As for Maggi, there was a lot of catching up to do. She knew that *Paradise Found* had long ago been succeeded by *Happy Families*, and then a series on how to make the best of your figure, your budget, your lifestyle, all of it presided over by a sparkling Maggi. She knew, too, that James had been succeeded by a Laurence, then a Sasha and others whose names now escaped her, as indeed did that of the latest. By the time Lorna had dealt with the queue, the supply of pâtés had all but run out and Maggi, her hand still being patted by Mum, had got herself under control.

Between them they loaded up the van with the empty trays, tucked Mum between them on the driver's bench seat and drove home.

While Mum had her afternoon nap, the two sisters settled at the breakfast bar in the kitchen and Maggi talked. And talked. One by one, she said, the men in her life had left: not because of any major dispute, but because work on a new series was taking them to a new location and, of course, they'd be back in touch as soon as …. Only it never happened. Or they'd made a decision to go back to the more humdrum but secure nine-to-five world of their peers. Or, occasionally, because they had simply met someone else. Then she paused and added "Or maybe none of them was ready for the slower track of commitment."

"Commitment puts a break on some ambitions," Lorna agreed.

"You and Bob seem to manage."

"Mm. But then I never was much into ambition."

"You seem to be managing very well without."

Lorna got up to fill the kettle. "Sometimes things just happen, if you let them."

"Yeah, but you need to have some talent or skill for things to happen with. Just look at your pâtés, and how things have worked out with those; and how marvellously you've coped with Mum." She paused, ran her fingers through her hair. "I guess a fair measure of unselfishness helps, too. I'm really proud of you, Sis."

Lorna plugged the kettle in, got down two mugs, inserted a teabag apiece. "I always was more suited to being a little fish in a big pond. But look at you with your series and shows, a household name. Mum gets such a kick out of seeing you on the box. So do I of course."

"And who remembers me half an hour after the show is over?"

"Now you're being silly. What about iplayers and ipods? Not to mention repeats. Anyway tell me what's on your schedule for the future? "

Maggi wrinkled her nose. "That's another question mark in my life. There's talk of some new reality series, taking the stars of various sitcoms and plonking them down in some very remote village somewhere in middle Europe with a limited amount of cash, and seeing how they get on. You know the sort of thing: the camera recording every twitch of a muscle. The idea is to see which of us adapts best to the circumstances into which they are bound to fling a few nasty surprises."

It sounded ghastly, but Lorna said cheerfully, "Well, it'll be a doddle for you. You've always been ace with people, and look how you used to get us out of scrapes as kids."

"I don't think falling into the local stream and being late for supper is quite in the same category," Maggi said soberly. "Anyway, for whatever reason, I suddenly yearn for normality …."

"… whatever that maybe…." they both chorused, and then grinned at each other.

As the cordless kettle began to shriek, Lorna got up and made the tea. "I'll take a cup up to Mum. She won't want to miss more of your visit than necessary. By the way, the granny-annexe is almost finished and partly furnished, including a put-me-up which is quite comfortable if you'd like to stay over. In fact, it would do us both a favour as you can give us some tips for tomorrow's interview."

They spent the evening discussing the ideas Lorna wanted to put over to Christopher Brent next day Several times Maggi interrupted with a suggestion or some re-phrasing. It was clear that she knew exactly what she was talking about and had a talent for imparting it to others. Then they primed Mum on what she should or should not say. It did not matter that she

214

would have forgotten it all by the time she went to bed. "I'll come with you," Maggi said, "then you can concentrate on what you want to say."

"Thanks, Sis," Lorna said, giving her a hug as she left her to settle down for the night.

Christopher Brent was brisk and business-like when they met in his office next morning. Interesting to see people in a different context Lorna thought. The rather diffident young man from the market was clearly at ease and in charge of a department humming with activity. Likewise, Maggi, seemed equally at home and much more her old self.

Mum, a little bemused by so much going on, behaved perfectly leaving it to 'the girls to sort everything out as they always do' as she confided to Christopher.

Having settled the details of how and when the programme would take shape, and the date for the first rehearsal, Christopher turned to Maggi. "You're a wow at this, aren't you?" he said. "I reckon you've been wasting your talents. In fact, I've been thinking we should do something similar for the young – you know the confused young who haven't quite sorted out what to do with the rest of their lives."

"Role play," Maggi said. "Give 'em some leads and let them work it out for themselves. You'll be surprised with what they come up with."

"I knew you'd have some good ideas." Christopher smiled. "Fancy expanding on them a bit, perhaps over dinner one evening? That is, if you're staying around for a while."

"Yeah," Maggi said. "I'd like that. And I guess I am."

"What a nice young man," Mum said as they went down in the lift.

"Isn't he?" Lorna agreed, and gave Maggi the sort of wink that was straight out of their long ago childhood.

----oOo----

Maggi and Christopher married a year later. It was too late for children, but they had a wow of a time world-travelling, lecturing, writing, broadcasting. Lorna's children transplanted themselves to remote parts of the world where she visited them, especially after Bob died of viral pneumonia, and until long distance travel became too tiring and a bit painful.

Fortunately Maggi (now reverted to Margaret) and Christopher settled only 20 miles away, and the sisters gradually re-discovered their inseparability. With no notice Christopher had died in his sleep one February night three years earlier.

Lorna did a lot of voluntary stuff for the village, including visiting oldies in Manorfields Care Home. After all, she was an oldie herself. So, in due course, it made sense that she and Margaret moved in there too.

PHOTO CALL

"So, who's that?" my great niece Bridget demanded prodding at the screen. She had decided to check out the new scanner for my p.c. with some old family photographs. We were in my room at Manorfields Care Home. A couple of years earlier I had moved in to one of the self-catering flats in the grounds, but more recently I had transferred to the main building, rather reluctantly aware of my greater need for support. Bridget, bless her, had taken to visiting me even more frequently. The care home is a great place but it's nice to see younger faces.

I glanced at her, noted the emerald nail varnish and matching hair streak without comment. Rising fourteen can be a confusing age. She had styled her hair in keeping with the current top pop groups, and merely succeeded in looking poignantly innocent. A few more years and she would be a stunner, I thought, and prayed she would not take after Jerry: Jerry Williams, my brother-in-law and Bridget's grandfather.

"Well?" prompted Bridget. She peered more closely. "Oh, it's only Granddad after all. Never knew he ever had a moustache."

I returned my attention to the photograph on the screen and was surprised by a gentle, sad lurch in the region of my midriff.

"He didn't," I said "That's your Great Uncle Michael. Your grandfather's brother in Australia. You're right, they are alike." Amazingly so to look at, if not in any other respect.

"Oh yeah," Bridget looked at me slyly. "Sounds as though you fancied him. According to Granddad he was a bit of a wimp."

"That he certainly isn't," I said firmly. "Or wasn't". Good Lord, it was nearly half a century ago that Michael had left for Australia, so who was to know what he was now?

----oOo----

I'd been eighteen, not so much older than Bridget was now. Jerry, then on the career ladder in marketing, and my sister Pam at business college, were already an item.

Pam had been - still was - a golden girl, a stunner like Bridget would be soon. Pleasant, dependable were probably fair descriptions of me and I was relatively content with that these days - though not then when I'd have given a lot for Pam's head-turning looks. Not because of Jerry though, thank you. Self assured, good looking Jerry, who knew exactly where he was going, had never been my sort.

So it had been startling to say the least to come across him one summer afternoon relaxing in the park and reading Rupert Brooke.

"Never thought of you as into poetry Jerry," I couldn't resist saying. Then, as he looked up with a crooked smile quite unlike Jerry's usual sardonic grin, I said "Oh...."

The smile widened. "My brother. I'm Michael, down from Uni."

"Hi," I said, relief outweighing surprise. Yes, I could see now he was quite a lot younger than Jerry. "And I'm Sally, his girl friend's sister. "

Michael looked thoughtful. "Which makes it sort of in the family, doesn't it? And worthy of modest celebration."

Over an Australian Shiraz in the newest wine bar in town, I learned he was just coming to the end of

218

an Arts degree . He added "A sad disappointment to my big brother who always wanted someone to kick a football with and later take the business world by storm." He paused. "And you? You're not at all like Pam."

"No," I said sadly, jamming my fingers through short dark hair. "I don't think one family could produce two Pams. Though," I added, "she's really nice as well as beautiful."

Michael said "I wasn't talking looks but ... sort of ... stillness."

Like a petrified rabbit? Time to change the subject. "So who are your favourite poets?" I asked.

Pam pulled a face when I reported the encounter and said   "Bit of a wimp by all accounts," foreshadowing Bridget's words so many years later.

"Meaning by Jerry's account I suppose," I said .

Pam looked surprised, then smiled "Ah, so that's how things are! Well, well."

And I could actually feel my own crossness bridging the years as I snapped "Things aren't like anything at all."

But might they have been, given a bit more understanding - perhaps maturity - on my part? We'd done a few tramps together through the Cotswold countryside, been to the odd gig. I hugely enjoyed Michael's easy and undemanding company in contrast with the let-it-all-hang-out of most of our peers, and was briefly disappointed when he didn't suggest keeping in touch when he headed north to a teaching job in Edinburgh.

By the following summer everyone was neck-deep in wedding plans. Pam was radiant, Jerry more pleased with himself than ever. Michael was to be best man, I bridesmaid.

I opened the door to him when he came round to discuss details, and he said laconically "Hi there. Looks as though it's up to you and me to get these two properly launched." And it was as if we'd only parted the previous day.

"You've grown a moustache," I said, and he laughed at my accusing tone and said "Not really me is it?"

The wedding was perfect. Pam looked fantastic, and even Jerry seemed briefly subdued by the momentousness of the occasion. After they had left for their honeymoon in the Canadian Rockies, Michael whisked me off for a meal. Over it we talked non-stop of our various activities and aspirations: my decision to do a computing course; Michael's take on teaching, followed by a run-down of Edinburgh's cultural scene. After that we dated regularly and the relationship seemed to take on a sense of pre-destiny that made me take more than I perhaps should for granted.

The following Easter Michael announced "I've had a fantastic offer to spend a year in Australia on an exchange scheme. Starting in September," He was almost jabbering in his excitement. Then he saw my expression. "Sorry I didn't really mean to blurt it out quite like that. But it's such a fantastic opportunity."

Looking back, I know I reacted like a child threatened by the loss of a favourite toy. I can even recall the petulance as I said "You're *taking* it?"

Michael looked astounded. "Of course I am." He'd taken my hands gently in his, repeating "It's such a fantastic opportunity." Then adding "I'll miss you dreadfully, you must know that; but it's only for a year."

And I'd pulled my hands away, snapping "And what am I supposed to do - put my life on hold?"

Presumably he assumed I'd come to see it from his perspective; instead a new and completely unfamiliar sense of insecurity corroded into festering resentment. Nothing had been resolved by the time he returned to Edinburgh, and nothing in his subsequent letters indicated any change of mind. My replies became ever more stilted and the gaps between them longer. Then a fellow student took pity on my misery and we did a few discos together. Childishly I hoped news of this would filter through to Michael and affect his decision.

It did not. A sad little note from Australia wished me happiness along whatever path I chose. Fortunately my computing course began soon after and I flung myself into it with manic single mindedness. Then Bridget was born and I gladly accepted the role of godmother.

Three years passed and Michael did not return. Correspondence dwindled to an exchange of Christmas messages. Boy friends came and went. Some were great company but none inspired any sense of commitment. Or perhaps it simply was that my own developing career as a software consultant triggered a greater one. It was still the relatively early days of new technology and I found it totally fascinating. And that I was good at it.

"Seems Michael's doing very well for himself in Oz. English lit. tutor at some University and researching early Australian diarists," Pam said once casually, then after a pause "I really thought you two were an item."

"Things change," I said shortly.

News came of his marriage to a young Australian writer and a few years later their separation. "Trust Michael to let such a peach go," was Jerry's comment. She had looked more like a model to me than a peach – or a writer, come to that – on the wedding pictures.

I was travelling much more, at first in the UK, then Europe and North America. And in-between I delighted in Bridget's evolution from baby- to little-girlhood to teenager to young wife and finally mother to my great niece also called Bridget.

----oOo----

"Did you know he's poorly," she asked now, as we scanned more recent photographs. "Granddad I mean. Cracked his head when a car went into the back of his."

No, I didn't know. Later I rang Pam to enquire, half expecting her to brush it off as a mere bump on the head. Instead an anxious voice said "I'm pretty worried Sal - he's got a blinding headache, can't stand light, and is getting more and more muzzy. Won't call the doc." Whatever else, Jerry was not a whinger. "But I've called him anyway."

By that evening Jerry was in hospital. Anxious hours extended into anxious days of waiting for the results of tests and scans. And finally the discovery of a clot and the decision to operate.

I arranged for Pam to pick me up on her way to the hospital. Whatever our differences, Jerry had made her happy and fathered a bright and beautiful daughter.

"We haven't always seen eye to eye," he said, drawn and subdued on the eve of the operation. "But you're a real friend to that granddaughter of mine. And I'd give my life for that sister of yours."

I said gently "I guess we're too alike. As in pigheaded! Let's try harder."

Much later I thought how amazingly the mind becomes concentrated in real crises. As we waited for

222

Jerry to come out of the operating theatre, it seemed the most natural thing in the world to look up tiredly from a magazine I was pretending to read and see Michael coming towards us.

"How glad I am to see you." Pam rose and held out her arms.

"I booked a flight as soon as I put the phone down from your call." Over her shoulder he smiled at me. "Hello there."

Maturity and a bronze tan suited him; he had aged very attractively. I said "You look well, Michael. Come to distract us with a breath of Upside Down Land?"

Moments later the Registrar came through to say the operation had been successful, that we must be prepared for recovery to be slow but there was no reason why it should not be complete. Forty-eight hours later we allowed ourselves to believe the worst was over.

After so much tension there was a kind of unreality about resuming normal routines. Perhaps it made it easier to come out with things that might have been better said long ago.

Sipping coffee in the day room, I heard myself say, "So in the end you settled for a more exciting life style?"

Michael made a wry face. "We were both very young and self-absorbed. I thought if I waited, you'd change your mind so only have myself to blame when you found someone else."

So my childish little ploy had backfired. I said, "It was all dire until life started sort of taking over again."

"Yes. Yes, it was."

223

"Still who knows - if I had changed my mind, perhaps you wouldn't have stayed in Australia and become so successful."

"And married that spectacularly beautiful little monster." Michael smiled ruefully. "Didn't I once tell you there are many different forms of beauty?" Fancy remembering that.

When we got back to the ward Bridget was sitting on her grandfather's bed while Pam arranged a vase of fresh flowers nearby. She turned smiling. "You'll be staying a while, Michael, now you're here? There's a room for you as long as you want."

"Thanks." Michael hesitated. "Fact is I'm coming up to retiremnent so I'm thinking of returning to th U.K. so this could be an opportunity to look around for a place." He was looking at me. "What do you think?"

Amazing how important that question seemed even after all this time. "I think," I said slowly "that Oz is a long way from your family. And old friends."

"That's what I was thinking too," Michael said.

Bridget looked at him slyly. "I could do with a nice groovy great uncle," she said.

Michael turned and winked at me. His expression indicated that he, too, thought his great niece was showing unrealistic expectations but that it was quite likely I could expect a new regular visitor at Manorfields in the future. And maybe even that Manorfields might have a new resident in due course.

THE DON'T CARE GENERATION

The early hours of the morning were always the worst. In her room at Manorfields Care Home Phillida flicked on the radio. A calm, well modulated voice announced that this was the BBC World Service with the news at three o'clock GMT. There followed fifteen minutes of gloom and doom. A Middle Eastern country was on the threshold of civil war; an overloaded ferry in the Far East had capsized with the loss of 200 lives; two opposing groups in central Africa were slaughtering each other; thanks to advances in forensic science a 40-year-old murder was about to be solved. Well, that was something anyway.

Phillida flicked off the radio. Hadn't someone once started a Good News programme and it had collapsed in weeks? People didn't want good news, it wasn't exciting. Power corrupts, absolute power corrupts absolutely. The same applied to fear. And bad news. Bad news triggered ever more bad news.

She glanced at her watch. Another fifteen minutes gone. Thank heavens Eleanor was on night duty. Give it another half-hour and she would press her bell. Eleanor would come in with a cup of camomile tea and, if she had time, stay for a short chat - and Phillida would feel better, another night overcome.

Odd how old age had crept up on her almost without her noticing. Gradually she had given up one responsibility and then another. The odd fall became a regular occurrence and her younger sister Ros had finally persuaded her to move into sheltered accommodation. She had transferrred to Manorfields three months ago when the falls and attendant visits to A&E became all too frequent.

Sometimes she wondered where all her anger had gone: the anger that had activated so much of her earlier life. It wasn't that she had enjoyed being angry. It was just that she couldn't bear the slovenly way things were done. The 'don't care' generation she called them, the youngsters who came within her orbit, whether it was cleaning the house, doing the garden, or working in the typing pool where she was supervisor by the time she reached twenty-five.

She knew the girls laughed at her: at her mousy hair and old fashioned appearance, and her precise way of talking. But for as long as she could remember, it had been important to her to take pride in what she did and to do it to the best of her ability. By the age of thirty she was in charge of a department in Better Sales, and by thirty-five its managing director. With time, the slovenliness of the young only seemed to get worse as far as she could see.

"No wonder you never married, Phil," Ros said after overhearing her telephone conversation with a junior. Ros was the only one who dared shorten Phillida's name to Phil.

They mutually respected each other, Ros and Phil: Ros for Phil's drive and efficiency; and Phil for Ros's charm and real niceness. Small wonder that Ros married in her early twenties, had four cherubic children by her early thirties. Less predictable was that she should be a widow by her early forties.

By then Phillida had done a course and was teaching the Africans the benefits of family planning, prior to giving the Malaysians and Bangladeshis similar benefits of her wisdom. No one bothered about her old fashioned appearance there; they were only interested in the fact that she got things done and that it made their lives just a little easier. No one noticed, least of all

226

Phillida herself that her mousy hair had turned to pepper-and-salt and finally to grey.

By the time she returned to Middle England for good, both sisters were in their sixties and Ros's children had turned into Dave the builder; Rob the DiY merchant; Mags the district nurse; and Pris the wannabe artist. Pris was the youngest, wildest, artiest. The other three were reasonably settled with, between them, sensible careers and five grandchildren for Ros. Pris, unmarried, was shortly to produce the sixth.

Ros herself had had a stroke and needed full time care in a pleasant but pricey institution where she was being rehabilitated. Her mind was as lively as ever, but her right side was frozen affecting her ability to do most things for herself. Pris went to see her every day growing visibly moore pregnant.

"Don't you worry about her?" Phillida couldn't resist asking.

Ros smiled her crooked smile. "I know you used to call them the 'don't care' generation, but they do, you know, especially for each other."

"Hm," Phillida said.

Phillida resumed her charity work, in due course becoming secretary to a support group for dysfunctional families and fund raiser for adopting third world grannies. There was no time for a social life and in any case she felt no need for it. She visited Ros from time to time and was delightedly amazed by her progress. Eventually Ros was released back into the world, spending brief visits in turn with each of her married children before returning to her home now fully equipped with gadgets to make life easier. Pris had decided to move back home and keep an eye on her.

Phillida visited her there on the eve of her own departure for an international conference in

Luxembourg on single-parent families. On her return there was a crisis with third world grannies, and then a series of launches to fund nursery care for the progeny of single parents. Not to mention the talks that took her to schools all around the county and beyond, promulgating the value of hygiene and safe sex. It was from one of these institutions no doubt that she picked up a bug that knocked her for six.

It was a virus, the doctor said. Nothing to be done but to stick it out. There was a particularly virulent one going about at the moment. Drink plenty and take paracetamol to keep her temperature down. For a week, Phillida lay in bed, alternately sweating and shivering. She did not even answer the door or the telephone.

Early on she rang the corner shop mini-market and asked them to deliver a consignment of invalid food in different flavours, which she mixed with water or milk. It was disgustingly cloying, but the packets told her she was imbibing the right balance of protein, vitamin and minerals. Periodically she picked up the mail, and eventually opened the front door to find two plastic bags of rubbish. People really were disgusting. She dumped them in her wheelie bin.

She had of course cancelled her commitments, but now began slowly to pick up the threads of normal life. Even working part time she was exhausted by the evening. Then the plastic shopping bags started appearing again. Irritably she plonked them in a box by the wheelie bin and hoped they would not attract rats . Finally she found the energy to go round and see Ros.

"Welcome stranger," her sister said, looking radiant, her smile now only very slightly crooked. She proceeded to demonstrate to Phillida how adept she now was at a whole range of household jobs, including preparing a meal.

"Why don't you stay?" she suggested. "Pris would love to see you and has been a tower of strength. She told me, by the way, how poorly you've been. I did try and ring…."

Phillida shrugged. "A minor bug. And how did Priscilla know that?"

"Oh that group of hers seem to know everything. Probably some of them have kids at one of those schools you talk to."

"Hm," Phillida said.

"Anyway, my dear, did you enjoy that mousse I made for you? One of my first efforts. It was in Pris's last food parcel."

Mousse? Food parcel? Phillida's mind raced and finally settled on a boxful of plastic shopping bags.

"Mm, I haven't got around to it yet," was all she could think of saying.

"Oh Phil. Well, don't leave it too long – there's real cream in it."

As soon as she got home, Phillida retrieved the plastic shopping bags. A nasty whiff came from one of them and she glimpsed strawberries well passed their 'use by' date. But the lemon mousse in a plastic container looked fine, as did a packet of ginger nuts, some camomile tea (how had Pris known that was her favourite?), a container of dried fruit, three tins of soup, a jar of peaches in brandy, and an interesting choice of boil-in-the-bag meals.

She felt a tightening of the throat as she took the bags into the kitchen and examined their contents. At the bottom of one was a note: *Hi Auntie Phil – Hope you soon feel better. Only three weeks to go now."*

Three weeks? Oh, the baby.

She thought of all the charity she had dispensed in remote corners of the world and blessed Pris for dispensing hers nearer home. Then she made a decision. She would drop the child a note and offer her services as a baby sitter.

She found she was humming to herself as she stored her bag of goodies away.

----oOo----

The baby was a boy - Thomas, Tommy, Tom, now doing A levels, learning incomprehensible things in computer technology. He even taught some of them to his Aunt Phil and showed her how to use a mobile phone. Pris had evolved from mother to mature student, done a series of NVQs and come to work at Manorfields. And had adopted her second name, Eleanor. It was never too late for a new beginning.

That's what Eleanor had said to her the other day. Why didn't she give talks about her interesting life to other Manorfields residents? It would help break up the day for all of them. In the process she could relive those wonderful memories.   And perhaps some of the other residents would feel like sharing theirs.

Mm, Eleanor was right. It was never too late.

STAYING WITH GRAN

"There's no alternative," Ma said.

Abby was awash with dismay. At a stroke, the post-GCSEs summer which had stretched ahead bright with promise of freedom was reduced to immeasurable greyness.

The fact that it was entirely her own fault did not make it any easier.

"You'll come a cropper with those absurd heels," Dad had said regularly before he left for that six month contract in Cape Town. It was small consolation that he wasn't there exuding *I told you so* that afternoon when a heel broke, sending her flying ungracefully across the shopping precinct to land at the feet of an old boy talking on a mobile. The pain in her right arm was excruciating.

The old boy had rung Ma who had chugged up in her Robin Reliant ten minutes later to whip her off to Casualty. "Fractured humerus," the young doctor on duty had said, sounding unnecessarily cheerful, and passed her on to a nurse for further ministration.

"That settles it," Ma said that evening. "There's no question of you staying at home on your own. Not even with neighbours keeping an eye on you."

Briefly remorseful, Abby protested "But you can't cancel your trip now."

"I've no intention of cancelling it," Ma said. "Dad's planned a full programme: safaris, whale watching, trekking in the Drakensbergs. We're not missing out because you insist on wearing absurd shoes. No, you'll have to stay with Gran."

Abby was aghast. "I'll die of boredom."

Ma's expression suddenly brightened. "No you won't. In fact, this could be a godsend. Remember Gran will be moving into Manorfields Care Home soon after we get back. You can help her sort out the things she wants to take, things she needs to get rid of. You could also start thinking about your future. And at least try and be gracious. Gran has always had a busy life, you know, and just now it will be even busier."

Like what? Knitting circles? Baking cakes, making jam? And being an eco-freak, she refused to have a car.

Desperately, but to no avail, Abby had contacted every friend and acquaintance she could think of. Now, a week later, she stared out of the coach window at the pleasant but distinctly ungroovy Midlands countryside. By now Ma would be dripping with sun oil on some South African beach. In fairness, she had tied up every conceivable loose end before she left: filled the fridge with meals to tide Abby over the couple of days before Gran could have her, alerted neighbours who had taken their 'keeping-an-eye-on-her' duties very seriously.

One of them had driven Abby to the bus station. "Your gran lives on her own?" she supposed. "It'll be nice for her to have company for a while."

No point in saying Gran was, reportedly, no more enthusiastic about the prospect of a grandaughterly visit than Abby. You'd think she'd be glad to have someone young around the place. The fact was that Abby, who had last seen her when she was eight or nine, remembered very little about her except that she seemed exceedingly old. That was the time Granddad had died somewhere out in Africa where he'd been an engineer or something and Gran came home on a visit to sort out his affairs.. A few months ago she'd come home for good. There'd been a lot of fuss about finding her a cottage in the country where Ma visited her quite regularly. But then Ma liked The Country. Abby was deeply suspicious of it, her memories being that it was full of things that bit or stung or scratched or made weird noises just when you thought you couldn't stand the silence any more.

It was an hour's drive, swaying and jolting down ever-narrowing roads. By the time Gran's village appeared on the signposts there were only two other people left on the coach. They passed alongside the high walls of some big estate, through a wood, between more fields, passed more cows, finally came into a winding village street with a small green and a pond.

As the coach pulled away, Abby surveyed her surroundings without enthusiasm. There were a lot of half timbered houses, an old pub, the square tower of a church. Picturesque it had to be said. And quiet as the grave: just a black and white cat cleaning itself on a wall outside the Thatched House Tearooms. *Thatched House Tearooms.* Yuck!

But where was the old girl? Abby checked the address – 16 High Street – and saw the nearest house was number 54. So it couldn't be far, and at least her suitcase had wheels.

Number 16 had roses scrambling over the porch. And, would you believe, the old girl had left the front door ajar! Through it, Abby caught the intermittent murmur of someone on the phone. She dumped her case in the small hallway and followed the sound into what was obviously a living room in the fullest sense of the word. She had never seen a room so crammed with furniture, ornaments, plants, books, scattered newspapers. It would clearly take forever to sort this lot out.

233

Then her attention was caught by the back of a large armchair and, waving above it, a gesticulating hand. A pair of legs clad in bootleg jeans hung over one of the chair arms, a sandal dangling from one big toe.

"Yes, I'll bring her along," a firm voice was saying. "She should be able to cope with a couple of miles. As far as I know her legs are all right, though I suspect she's a townie through to her no-doubt purple toenails…." A pause. "Lord knows, Denzel – haven't seen her since she was eight, nine, and she was precocious enough then. Dare say I'll have my head caving in with jungle music by Screech or Smell or whatever the latest group is." Another pause. "No, it's today she's arriving. On the three o'clock bus …. Oh my God."

The legs disappeared, a slight figure rose into view running a hand through short, wild tawny hair. Blue eyes met Abby's hazel ones. "Oh my God," Gran said again and dropped her mobile.

"It's Blur," Abby said. "The name of my favourite group. And, like, what you call jungle music, that's probably ragga, or maybe hip-hop. It's really cool. I could tell you about it if you like." She shrugged and added "And, s'ppose, you could tell me about country stuff, while we're sorting out your things."

Gran managed to look sheepish, welcoming and interested all at the same time. "I suppose," she agreed, "there's a lot we have to learn about each other after all these years. You probably don't know that I used to do the music halls in my young days. I was a Bluebell Girl. Father - that's your great grandfather - was horrified. But I was a bit of a rebel. Perhaps a bit like you? We might have quite a lot in common," she finished hopefully."

"What's a Bluebell Girl?" Abby asked.

"A chorus girl. Not your sort of music." Gran paused. "But you might find it interesting?" she suggested.

"Yeah," Abby said, and began to think that just maybe she might.

IT'LL BE BETTER TOMORROW

"We could put that on your gravestone," I said, reaching for the chopping board.

"What?" Ben asked. He was perched on the high stool provided by the National Health Service; it had become routine that he came in to the kitchen to watch me prepare supper.

"'It'll be better tomorrow'" I quoted. "You say it every day." *Countless times every day.* "Get me a couple of peppers from the fridge, would you? And two aubergines – oh, and .... " I stopped. The Memory Clinic nurse said you shouldn't expect them to remember more than two things. Them. People who had short term memory loss. With early stages of dementia.

Ben slid off the stool "What colour peppers? Are you doing a ratty thing?"

"Ratatouille, yup. One yellow, one red, please."

"Two aubergines… What else?"

"Courgettes, four." Ben arranged them in order of size along the kitchen counter and returned to his stool and newspaper.

"Isn't that what that comedian said – Spike Thingummy? 'It'll be better tomorrow'?"

"Spike Milligan. No, I think he said 'I told you I was ill.'"

"That's much funnier." Ben threw back his head and roared a real laugh that came from the belly. How often he had used that to diffuse a tense situation, especially with the children. Both of them were grown up, parents themselves now and scattered: New South Wales (Rob), Brussels (Dee). Well, Brussels wasn't so

236

very far, but too far to ask *could you just pop over, love, and sit with your Dad while I go to a meeting?*

Anyway, Dee wasn't the popping in kind, and there weren't any meetings nowadays.

"There won't be a gravestone, I'm being cremated," Ben pointed out. He hummed tunelessly while I chopped up onion, peppers, eggplant, courgettes. Then he asked, "Do you remember that time we were canoeing in Eastern Europe?" I was accustomed to the gymnastics of his mind and this was safe territory. He had total and almost uncanny recall of all our early adventures. What he didn't register was that there was no longer an Eastern Europe, just one big Europe that was a bit wobbly in places. "There was that fellow at the Hungarian border."

"Which fellow?" Sometimes his recall was way better than mine.

"The one who asked if we were hiding a stowaway. In a canoe, I ask you!" Ben gave another mighty roar.

I paused in my chopping. "I remember. I found an old English shilling and gave it to him for his coin collection."

"Decimalisation – 1971." Sometimes Ben's recall was quite eerie. It was the year they had decided to canoe the Danube from Vienna to Budapest. Rob had gone on a Scandinavian trek with the school, Dee was with Ben's Mum. The Hungarian soldier, who had poked around the canoe looking for stowaways, had fingered the English shilling with reverence. Funny how a shilling sounded much more valuable than 5 p.

----oOo----

We had met canoeing. He had been our instructor I was seventeen, Ben twenty-three and lean

237

and athletic and the whole sixth form was in love with him. I fell in the canal on the first day and he was the only one who didn't laugh.

It was 1951. Our generation was just easing itself out of post-war austerity and hadn't yet realised that All We Needed was Love. Looking back, it was a quaint courtship, with no thought of experimental Movings-in Together. We married three years later, Ben then comfortably on a banking careers ladder, while I was at the learning end of a small publishing outfit meeting local needs. Our son was born in July 1954, yelling so lustily that Ben named him Rob on the principle that we were about to be robbed of all future sleep. He tended to make cringing puns but I was too thrilled and relieved to protest, so the name stuck. But in fact he was to rob us of very little sleep: a placid baby he grew into a quiet, introspective toddler which might have been more worrying if he had not been pronounced healthy in all respects. By the time he had progressed from crawl to wobbly walk and finally deeply thoughtful potter, Dee was on the way. She did rob us of sleep, was terribly bright and let everyone know it.

It troubled me that I couldn't reach Rob, or whoever was there behind that closed little face. Later, when the face was still closed but not so little and he had found himself through computers, I was no nearer reaching him.

"No probs," Ben told me many times. using the expression he had picked up from Dee's Antipodean travels. "Rob has found his purpose in life and is OK. Anyway you should be the first to understand. Rob maybe married to a computer, but you're married to a telephone."

It was a standing joke. Ben hated the phone which he deemed to be the invention of the devil. True I did use it a lot - or did. Once the kids had gone to live their grown up lives, get married, have kids of their own, and my publishing outfit seemed to take care of itself, I became a committee junkie - Parish Council, local newsletter, website, nature reserve, neighbourhood watch.

It was a neighbour called Henry who had started Rob off on computers. "Remember that computer guy that used to live next door?" Ben asked. Even dementia hadn't removed our knack of recalling the same memory simultaneously.

"Henry," I said. "I was just thinking about him."

It was soon after their golden wedding anniversary that I noticed Ben's lapses of memory were beginning to seem more serious than absentmindedness. Initially there were trivial incidents: the car temporarily misplaced on a supermarket forecourt; an appointment missed; telephone messages that were not passed on. Then Ben had his first fall. That was the most disconcerting. I returned from shopping to find him sprawled by the half open side door.

"Thought I might get help from a passerby," he said cheerfully, having dragged himself there after falling off the sofa.

On that occasion a young neighbour heaved Ben to his feet, but in due course we graduated to paramedics and A. & E. Hours and hours in A & E.

Then Rob paid one of his biannual visits. "Pa losing it a bit," he stated rather than asked rather soon. "How about down-sizing? Or a retirement home. There's that Manorfields place only a few miles away."

"He gets tired," I admitted. "But we like this place." After several moves we had settled on a modern executive house in a less fashionable part of the Cotswolds, four bedrooms, one en suite, two providing an office each. I spent most of the day in mine, promoting, blogging, socialising, petitioning for this or that good cause. Once retired, Ben pottered in the garden but spent increasingly more time dozing over a book or listening to music.

It was during that visit that he had several falls. Rob rang Dee who came over and reinforced the down-sizing argument. Before returning to their busy lives they extracted a promise that we would think about it.

The shock was greater than we would admit. Despite a sedentary job, Ben had always been supremely fit, the canoeing supplemented then replaced by regular sessions at the gym and running.

One evening I returned from a meeting. "I can't move," Ben complained. He could, but with difficulty. Sadly, I watched him negotiate the stairs.

Eventually he was diagnosed with polymyalgia rheumatica and put on steroids. A few weeks later a heart murmur required warfarin, and later a weird blood condition added further medication to the list. Rob and Dee arrived mob-handed with spouses.

There were several visits to Manorfields. We had to admit the staff were lovely. "And it's right in the middle of he village," Dee pointed out. "Near the bus stop and the Co-op. And the pubs where Dad could meet his friends. You could start off in one of their flats in the grounds. They're really well equipped and you'd still have your independence,"

It all made such good sense, and I carefully did not dwell on the reference to 'you could start off'.

"And what about my books?" Ben demanded. Three living room walls were floor-to-ceiling bookcases, jam packed.

I almost envied Ben his short-term memory loss. When Rob, Dee and spouses departed he apparently put the whole disconcerting business out of mind. I simply went on worrying away at the future.

For a while it seemed as though the kids had put it out of mind, too. Rob was heavily involved in expanding his IT software company across Australasia. Dee and her husband were coping with a sudden explosion of teenage angst and had moved from Brussels to Strasbourg. It didn't seem necessary to tell them of Ben's increasing falls, or the collapsed lung, or several other briefly worrying 'health issues', as our G.P. called them.

And then he had a pulmonary embolism, and down-sizing was back right at the top of the agenda. A three-room flat was coming on the market at Manorfields with plenty of wall space for book cases, and a secluded feel near a patch of woodland away from the main building. I started to feel fractionally more hopeful.

Things began to happen at breakneck speed. The house went on the market and sold almost immediately to a young couple with two small children. Dee made lists and we went systematically through each room noting what was for auction, for social housing, for charity, for recycling. Especially recycling. Dee and Rob loaded the car and it was my task to drive to the recycling centre where I watched much of the evidence of our lives being hurled on to landfill, sometimes the tears streaming down my cheeks. Thankfully Ben agreed to a week of respite care where I visited him daily, putting on a brave face, censoring out some of the harder decisions.

"M-u-u-m!" I recognised the tone. Something didn't match up to Dee's high standards. "These knives ... they don't cut!"

"No, Love. Your Dad doesn't do much knife-sharpening these days."

Dee went shopping and returned with a set of sparkling cut-throat knives. And a mobile telephone. Apparently ours was rubbish, too.

"It's OK, OK," she said. "I've got you a really simple one."

I looked at its menu (since when did telephones have menus?): email, internet, camera, apps.....

With Rob things were different. Things weren't rubbish, or at least he didn't say so. They were just all in the wrong place, or well passed their use-by date, or no longer relevant, or maybe a bit on the grubby side. Well, it was true that house cleaning didn't have the priority it once had. Rob bought a white board on which to crayon the week's appointments. Insidiously the list had grown: carers, cleaner, social worker, district nurse. Everyone told me how wonderful I looked for my age. I didn't feel wonderful. I wished everyone would go away and knew it wasn't going to happen. They left with assurances that they would be back asap.

And then our young purchasers hit a snag in their own house sale and there was a delay. Possibly some weeks. Rob's presence was urgently needed in New Zealand at a newly opened office. Dee said it was time she checked up on the family.

On the eve of their departure, they produced a list in duplicate of jobs for us: the labelling of an enormous number of boxes according to contents and for which room, charity, auction they were destined. Dee had her car and drove Rob to the airport before heading for the cross-channel ferry.

We stood on the doorstep waving them off, Ben leaning heavily on his walking frame. When we closed the front door behind us, the house felt eerily quiet.

The kitchen looked immaculate, the breakfast things put away. On the counter, Dee had made a list of menus for the next days, all labelled in the top of the freezer.

Ben stood looking at me with that intuitive look that continued to outlive his decline. "What's up?" he asked.

I shrugged helplessly. "It's all a bit ... a bit overwhelming," I said and burst into tears

Ben put his arms round me and gave me one of those hugs that makes my world feel completely safe and impregnable, even though I know it isn't. Then he stood back and smiled that smile that had won me over all those years ago.

"Mm." he said. "It'll be better tomorrow, you know," then added "Even several tomorrows."

And I smiled back because on this occasion I really thought he could be right.

What other people say ....

Preview of It'll be Better Tomorrow: *Poignant, and intensely human stories. You feel you know the people Sylvie Nickels writes about.* Ian Mathie, Author of the African Memoir series.

Reviews

Another Kind of Loving: *.... this hooked me in and wouldn't let go until ... the last page.* The Bookbag.co.uk

Beyond the Broken Gate: *.... powerful, far-reaching* Four Shires magazine

Long Shadows: *... brought Sarajevo home to me in a way that no amount of media coverage has ever done.* The Bookbag.co.uk

Lightning Source UK Ltd.
Milton Keynes UK
UKOW04f0812020915

257887UK00002B/22/P